Custom Built deals with topics some readers might find difficult, such as cancer and pregnancy loss.

CUSTOM BUILT

———

CHANTAL FERNANDO

carina
press

carina press®

Recycling programs
for this product may
not exist in your area.

ISBN-13: 978-1-335-20013-6

Custom Built

This edition published by arrangement with Harlequin Books S.A.

For questions and comments about the quality of this book, please contact us at CustomerService@Harlequin.com.

Carina Press
22 Adelaide St. West, 40th Floor
Toronto, Ontario M5H 4E3, Canada
www.CarinaPress.com

Printed in U.S.A.

For my firstborn son,

Your soul is rare, and your heart
is made of pure gold.

Which is why I'll always be here
to protect you.

I love you.

CUSTOM BUILT

Prologue

Bronte

"I'm afraid the abnormal cells have returned, so you will need another surgery."

I stare at my doctor. His kind face used to bring me hope, and now it is delivering the worst kind of news.

A year ago, my health wasn't something I had worried about; I was perfectly healthy. Then one abnormal pap smear changed my life.

I was hopeful that after my last surgery, I'd be given the all clear. But nope. Here I am, listening to my doctor tell me I need yet another surgery. I try to keep myself composed, but the truth is that I'm scared shitless.

"Is that really necessary?"

"I'm afraid so. It will only take about twenty minutes. It's the loop electrosurgical excision procedure and we don't even have to put you fully under. It'll be just a local anesthetic."

The memory of my last procedure is scarred on my brain. I remember the smoke filling the room, I remember the smell of it burning the cells away. It may have only been twenty minutes, but it is something I never wanted to have to experience again.

"I remember."

He hasn't used the word *cancer* yet, but if these abnormal cells continue to return, it can turn into cervical cancer.

"Bronte…" Dr. James hesitates. "We can keep going in and doing these surgeries every time the cells return, but there are other options, other surgeries. Ones that will allow you to live your life without these tests or living in fear that they will return."

"Well, sign me up for that!" No more tests, no more visits to Dr. James, kind face and all. No more fear.

"It's a hysterectomy."

As he says the words, I feel the air leave me. I'm nowhere near ready for children, but I want the option to have them. "That seems a little extreme, no?"

"We need to do what we can to make sure you don't get cervical cancer."

And there it is. Cancer or children.

"Okay, let's do the surgery. If we need to consider the hysterectomy, then I'm open to it, but only if it's necessary. Whatever we need to," I say, swallowing hard.

I'm not ready to leave this world yet. I haven't even left my mark on it.

After I schedule my surgery, I leave to go to work, but my head is reeling from everything. My dad calls me as soon as I get back into my car. "Hey, Bronte, how are you?"

His soothing voice calms me. Closing my eyes, I rest my head against the seat and take a deep breath. "I'm fine, Dad," I lie. "How are you? Are we still having lunch this week?"

My dad and I have always been close, but we became even closer after my mom passed away when I was ten. It's always been me and him against the world, and I can't imagine it any other way.

"Yeah, of course. Are you sure that you're fine, because you don't sound it," he murmurs, calling me out on my lies.

I'm silent for a few seconds. "The abnormal cells have returned and I need another surgery to remove them."

His breath hitches. "It will be fine, Bronte," he assures me. "I read up on all of this last time, and sometimes they come back, but they always catch them in time. You're lucky that it hasn't gotten past this stage."

His logic calms me.

I don't tell him about the conversation my doctor had with me about the hysterectomy.

I need time to process that for myself.

We chat for a while, him assuring me that everything will be fine and that he's here for me, and we will get through this together, and then I go back to work, like nothing happened.

I don't tell anyone else about my upcoming surgery, or about how for a month to six weeks I can't so much as go in a swimming pool until I recover.

I don't tell anyone else anything. I choose to suffer in silence instead.

Little do I know, sometimes when you hold things in, they have their way of eating you from the inside out.

Chapter One

"I'm sorry, Bronte," Nadia says, shoulders hunching. "You know how much the business has been struggling for months, and now it's barely making enough money for me to cover my own ass, never mind have an employee. I'm so sorry."

"It's okay," I tell her, forcing a smile, even though I feel like crying. I mean, I knew this was coming. I've worked as an assistant for Nadia's private investigator firm for years now, and I know how hard this decision must be for her. We had spoken about it a few months ago, and to be honest I'm surprised she has kept me on for this long.

However, that doesn't mean it doesn't hurt. I need this job, and I don't know what the hell I'm going to do without it. I don't have any other qualifications, and I can't afford to go back to college to finish my teaching degree. And I don't even want to talk about health insurance. Thank God I had my second surgery several months ago. I can't even fathom what I will do if the abnormal cells come back.

I know how bad times are for Nadia, though,

with us getting less and less work with every passing month. I'd spent this week cleaning and rearrang-
ing the office because I didn't have much else to do.

I see Nadia more like family than my boss, but I
know that she has to do what's best for her. I understand that—it's just going to be a shit time for me
right now.

"I'll pack up my things," I say, and swallow hard,
looking at my desk. I pick up the picture of me and
my dad, both of us smiling, his arms wrapped around
me. It was taken last year at Christmas, my red lipstick all over his cheek where I had kissed him. Dad
has always been my rock, and I know he'd help me if
I need it, but I'm too old to be running to my daddy. I
need to sort this all out myself and find a new job as
soon as possible, before my savings dry up and put
me in deeper shit.

"I'm really sorry," Nadia repeats, her voice crack-
ing.

I put the photo frame down and turn to give her a
hug. "It will be fine, it's not the end of the world. I'll
find another job, and hopefully business will pick up
for you and you can keep this place running."

This might not be what I need right now, a kick
when I'm down, already stressed out over my health
issues, but you can't control what curveballs life decides to throw you.

No matter what happens, I know I'll be okay.
When one door closes, another one opens, right?

I comfort Nadia, I gather my things, and I leave.

I woke up this morning employed and fairly optimistic, and now I'm going home without a job and no idea where my next paycheck is going to come from.

Life can be a bitch sometimes, can't it?

Just before Christmas isn't the best time to try to find employment. Everyone has already been hired for the season, and no one wants to take on someone they would have to train during the busy festive season. Not surprisingly, my resume isn't remarkable, and my private investigator skills aren't even going to help me work in a bar or restaurant.

"Have you ever worked in a bar before?" a manager at one of the establishments asks me.

"Well, no, but—"

"I'm sorry," he says, cutting me off. "We need someone with experience."

"I'm a fast learner."

I mean, how hard could it be, right? It's not like I'm a doctor looking for a new job. I can learn to serve drinks and food and wear a smile while doing it. I'm a hard and efficient worker; I just need someone to give me a chance. I didn't finish college because the timing wasn't right for me.

"Come back after the holidays" is all I get in response.

I decide to call up all the private investigator firms in my city, but none of them are hiring either. In the world of easily accessible technology, people are probably handling their own investigating, cutting out the middleman and leaving me jobless. I really hope Nadia will be okay and not have to shut down the firm. The thought saddens me, and I hope there's a way she can stay open and get more clients in the upcoming weeks. Otherwise she might be here along with me, trying to get any job she can.

My phone rings, "All I Want for Christmas Is You" playing loudly. "Hello?"

"Hey, princess," my dad says, and I can hear the smile in his tone. "I haven't heard from you in a week. Is everything okay?"

I haven't spoken to him since I got fired, because I don't want to admit that I'm currently failing at life. Asking for help has never been my strong point—I prefer to suffer in silence and try to solve all problems on my own. I know I'm going to have to tell him, though; I'm just going to buy myself a little time.

"Everything is fine, Dad," I assure him. "How are you?"

My dad lives about an hour away from my apartment, and we catch up for family dinner every week or so. Besides that, we usually text or chat every day or every other day. I love spending time with him, and I look forward to seeing him. Yes, I'm a daddy's girl.

"I'm good, just busy with work. You know how it is," he says.

Actually, right now I don't.

My dad has always worked hard, and that's where I got my own work ethic from. As soon as I was old enough to get a job, I did. I was never spoiled, and had to work for everything I had. For my first car, he told me he'd match whatever I saved, which taught me how to work for my money, but also allowed him contribute.

Dad now owns a construction business, along with my uncle Neville, who also owns and runs a farm. Dad mainly does the admin side of things, but he started off as a laborer, so he isn't afraid of hard work.

"I've been thinking about you today, so I thought I'd give you a call."

"When are you free this week?" I ask. Might as well face him, because avoiding him isn't going to help the situation. I can't lie to him, though, so I guess I'm just going to have to tell him what happened in person. Or maybe I should try to secure a new job first.

"Always free for you," he says, voice gentle. "I was actually calling to invite you over on the weekend. I'm having a barbecue, and everyone will be there. Your uncle wants to see you too, so I hope you can make it."

"Okay, message me the details and I'll be there," I reply. "I'm looking forward to it."

We say our byes and I love yous and hang up. Sighing, I glance down at my handful of resumes and lift my chin. Surely there's something for me out there. I'm too old to have no job security, and it annoys me that it has come to this. I should have gone back and finished my degree—then I'd have something to fall back on—but there's no point with the what-ifs now. I just need to find something, anything, and if I don't like it, I can always just stay in that job until I find something better.

"Who knows? In a few weeks I might have to come apply here," I mutter to myself as we pass Toxic, a well-known strip club.

If I didn't think my father would kill me, I might even consider it.

I spend the rest of the day handing out my resume, smiling and trying to act as charming as can be.

Just hoping the next door to open for me will be a good one.

Chapter Two

"Hey, princess," Dad says, opening his arms wide, smile etched across his face. I've barely gotten out of my car before I'm in his arms. I'm his only child, and he absolutely adores me, and I know that. The feeling is mutual.

"Hey," I say resting, my cheek against his chest. "How are you? You're looking nice." He's wearing a thin blue sweater I got him for his last birthday.

"Thank you." He beams. "Come on, let's go inside."

"There's a lot of people here," I say, frowning as we step through the door and walk through the house.

"The whole family, plus some friends of mine," he explains, resting his arms on my shoulders and looking at me. "You're a sight for sore eyes, you know that? I've missed you. I haven't really seen you since after the surgery."

"I'm fine, Dad," I assure him. "There's nothing to worry about anymore. It's all over with, and I just have to go back in a few months for a checkup."

Where hopefully they will find out that the cells haven't returned.

"I know, I know. I worry about you, though. You need to come and see me more. You know you could save so much money on rent and bills if you moved back in here. It's a bit of a drive to work, but it's not too bad. It would still save you a lot of money."

I smile at his familiar words. "I know, Dad. But I'm a grown woman, and I like being independent. I'm too old to be living with my dad and letting him pay for things for me."

"You could never be too old," he grumbles. I eye the food as we pass the kitchen table, all the salads and sides making my mouth water.

"Yum. You're right, maybe I will move home."

My dad is an amazing cook, which is a good thing because he had to take over being both the mother and father after Mom passed away. He raised me on his own ever since, and he did a damn good job at it, too. I remember he used to come to all the Mother's Day events at the school, being the only man there and not giving a shit, because he didn't want me to sit there and be alone.

He chuckles. My head turns when I hear the sliding door open.

"Uncle Neville," I say, smiling and giving my favorite uncle—okay, only uncle—a hug. "Long time no see. How have you been?"

"I've been good," he says, giving me a tight squeeze. "How about you? How's work been?"

Shit.

"Ummm…" I trail off, not wanting to tell them the truth, but not wanting to lie, either. On the drive here, I knew I was going to have to tell Dad about being fired, but thinking about it and actually doing it are two different things. I don't want him to worry, but I don't want to disappoint him either. I know he was very proud of me for having this job and would tell all of his friends how his daughter was a private investigator.

My dad picks up on my hesitation straight away. "What's happened? Did you get a bad case or something? I can help if you're in any trouble."

He is always there for me and has my back no matter what, which I really do appreciate, but sometimes it gets a little suffocating. I need to work things out for myself.

Sighing, my shoulders hunching, I decide to just get over it and tell them. "Actually the business is struggling, so Nadia had to let me go."

"Why didn't you tell me?" Dad asks, brow furrowing. "Do you need money? I can transfer some to you."

"I'm telling you now; it only happened the other day. And no, I don't need any money. I want to figure it out on my own," I tell him. I hate that I'm keeping things from him. Between this and the possible hysterectomy, I'm breaking our promise to be honest with one another. I know I should just tell him, but I don't want him to worry or to have to think about the fact that he might never be a grandfather. At least not biologically. It already breaks my heart that I won't be able to carry my own child, and I don't want to share the misery. Not yet, at least.

"If you're looking for a job, I know a place that's looking for someone," Uncle Neville pipes in, his amber eyes kind. I've always loved the color of his eyes, whereas Dad and I missed that gene and got dark brown instead.

"Where?" I ask, perking up. "No one seems to be hiring now. I've been submitting my resume for the last few days and there's been nothing so far."

He nods. "It's at a custom motorcycle shop. They had someone lined up for the holidays, but she bailed, so they're looking for someone new. All you have to do is man the cash register, answer phones. Typical admin work. What do you think? Something you might be interested in? I know they would pay pretty well."

I'm not opposed to doing any admin work, and anywhere is a start. It's not the type of place I'd usually apply at because I know nothing about their business, but beggars can't be choosers, and I really just want to get a steady income coming in again. Working behind a desk would probably be better than a bar, and I won't have to deal with drunk idiots every day, too. Is this a good idea? I don't know yet. But an opportunity has presented itself, and I'm going to take it.

"Yeah, very interested. I can do that. I know nothing about motorcycles, though."

"You can learn," he replies, shrugging as he slides his phone out of his jeans pocket. "I'll call them now and let them know."

"What? Just like that? I don't have to do an interview or anything?" I ask, frowning. "Who owns the shop?"

He's a very mysterious man—there's more than meets the eye with him. He has terrible taste in women, that I know, but luckily he and Georgia, his former wife, are over now. I don't know much about what happened with them, but I think she left him or something.

"Some friends of my daughter," he says casually, watching my reaction.

I glance between him and my dad. "Daughter?"

What? As far as I know, Neville only has a step-daughter, Skylar. We've hung out a couple of times, and she is a really cool chick. But we've been busy and haven't had a chance to catch up in a while.

"Did you knock someone up since we last talked? When did all of this happen? What else have I missed?"

Dad stands next to me and wraps his arm around me. "He didn't know about her until recently, and no, she's not a baby. She's around your age. Her name is Abbie. I saw a picture of her; she has Neville's eyes."

My mouth opens and closes. I don't even know what to say right now. "Who is her mother? How did you find out? I think I'm going to need a stiff drink."

So I have a cousin on my dad's side. I mean, I have Skylar too, but it's different since we never spent that much time together growing up. Her mom never really allowed that; maybe because we aren't blood related she didn't think it was important. But now Uncle

Neville has a daughter we all didn't know about, and now she's about to hook me, the cousin she's never even met, up with a job.

Wonderful.

I'm sure she's going to have a great first impression of me. I haven't even met her and I'm already calling in a favor.

I've always wanted that family connection, and ever since my mother died, I've only had my dad and my uncle. There's never been anyone my age, or any female influence around me. The thought that I could have that closeness now with Abbie makes me feel hopeful.

We all head outside and I say hello to everyone else, all my dad's good friends who have been around our family since I can remember. Plate of food in hand, I find a quiet spot in the corner and sit down when my dad finds me.

"You all right?" he asks, tone gentle. "I'm glad you came here today."

"I'm fine," I reply, looking down at my plate. "And me too. I'm a little bummed about my job, but you know these things happen. And I'm still processing the whole Abbie thing."

"Aren't we all," Dad murmurs. "He's going to bring her around soon, so if you could be here, that would be great. She really wants to meet us, but couldn't come today because she had something going on. She doesn't have much family."

"I'd love to meet her. How do you feel about having a niece?" I ask.

I'm still in shock about the whole thing, but in a good way. I've always wanted a bigger family, and now I have someone around my age. I hope the two of us will hit it off and be close. I've always wished I had a sibling, but it's not like that's going to happen, so a cousin is second best. It will be nice to have someone else I can call cousin.

"I feel…good. And I haven't seen my brother this happy in a long time, so it's really nice to see," Dad says, smiling to himself. "He's always been the best big brother to me, and he deserves the world, so it makes me happy to see him so happy. I always thought he'd make a wonderful dad."

"That's cute," I say, nudging him playfully with my shoulder. "She does have a great dad, and an amazing uncle, too. I can't wait to meet her."

"I have a good feeling about it all," he says, bringing his brown eyes to me. "Everything happens for a reason."

He's always thought that and had an optimistic outlook on life, even though he lost his wife, which has always puzzled me a little. Instead of becoming bitter and cynical at the world, he has always been the glass-half-full type of man, and I love that about him. It's how I try to look at the world as well.

"And about your job, you should have called me," he adds after a few seconds of silence. "You know that's what I'm here for. There's no reason for you to stress out and take it all upon yourself."

"I know, Dad," I say. "But it's fine. It's not the end of the world."

"If you need money—"

"I will let you know," I say, reaching out and touching his shoulder. "I know that you are here for me no matter what, okay? And if I get into deep shit, you're the first person I will call."

And that's the truth. But that doesn't mean I want to depend on him for everything. He wants to make my life easier, but I want to do the same for him, and that means not burdening him with all of my problems.

"Now what's been going on with you? Met any nice women?" I ask, changing the subject.

His eyes light up with humor. "None worthy of bringing home to you."

"You know I wouldn't care if you met someone and moved on with your life, Dad. Second loves are a real thing," I say.

"I know." He nods, sobering. "Your mom was my soul mate, Bronte. And there is no moving on from that."

"You don't have to find something the same—you could find something different, but still special," I say, resting my head on his shoulder. "It's just you here. Wouldn't you like someone to share a home with?"

Uncle Neville comes over and sits with us before my dad can respond. "All sorted for your job, Bronte. They will contact you and give you all of the information."

"You work fast. Thank you so much, that's a huge

stress relief," I say, giving him a warm hug. "I owe you one."

He squeezes me tightly and then cups my cheek before letting me go. "You owe me nothing. You're smart and a hard worker; they will love you there. You will probably get to see Abbie here and there too, because her partner is one of the owners," he explains.

"I hope so. I want to thank her in person and get to know her. It's not every day you find out you have a cousin who's the same age as you."

"I think you two will get on like a house on fire," he says. "I might not have been around to raise her, but she's a fine young woman. She is strong willed and has a good heart, just like you."

"So you had no idea about her?"

He shakes his head. "Her mom didn't tell me she was pregnant, so no, I had no idea until the truth came out."

"I'm sorry she did that to you," I say, brow furrowing. "But better late than never, right? At least we all get to know her now, and have her in our lives."

"Exactly," Dad adds, looking at his brother. "All that matters is now."

"I have a lot of time to make up for," my uncle admits, glancing out at the sky. "But yeah, I feel really lucky to have her in my life. I never thought I'd have any biological children."

"She's a lucky girl," I say, winking. "I'm going to go and grab a drink. Do either of you want anything?"

They decline. I get up, head back to the kitchen, put my plate away and grab a soda for myself. When

I come back outside, I see my dad and Neville in the corner together, chatting away. Whatever they're talking about seems pretty important, so I linger for a little while before returning to join them.

"That would be one million in profit; we'd be stupid to turn that down," I hear Neville saying to my dad as I finally approach. The two of them go silent at my arrival, the conversation cutting off.

"I can come back," I say, wondering what the hell they were talking about for that amount of money. I know my uncle is pretty well off and my dad does just fine, but that conversation makes no sense to me.

"No, don't be silly, come and sit with us," Dad says, tapping the spot next to him, where I was sitting before. "Your uncle can tell me about his business deals later."

I stay until it gets dark, and then head home. And the next morning, I get a message from someone named Crow. No phone call, just a text.

You start tomorrow. Be at Fast & Fury Custom Motorcycles by 10.

And just like that, my employment issues are over.

After glancing at the GPS on my phone, I park my car and look at the sign through my window. Yep, this is the place.

I wasn't joking when I said I didn't know a thing about motorcycles. My knowledge of cars, or any kind of vehicle for that matter, is pretty limited. I just hope

I can do a good job, because the last thing I need to do is make my uncle and the cousin I haven't met yet look bad for recommending me. I'm not going to lie, I'm feeling a little nervous right now, but I need to act confident and make a good impression.

Sliding out of the car, I pull down my knee-length pencil skirt and square my shoulders. The new material of my crisp white shirt isn't the comfiest, but it makes me look the part. As I pass the window to the entrance, I take a look at myself. With my long dark hair piled on my head in a bun and the glasses on my face, I kind of look like a librarian, but I guess that's a professional look.

Stepping inside the warehouse is like a whole other world. There's beautifully done graffiti on the walls, and the workspace shows off brand-new, sparkling bikes. The main room leads into a wide spacious garage, and it has a cool, urban vibe. There's music playing over the speakers, and it doesn't look like they have spared any expense with the interior design. In the middle, there's a reception area with a large, expensive-looking wooden desk and a little staircase leading to another level, one with bikes in various states of being rebuilt. It's a pretty awesome space.

"Hello?" I call out when I see no one around. Apparently they really do need staff. I'm assuming I'm supposed to be meeting Crow, but I have no idea what to expect right now.

A door opens from behind the reception area, and a tall, muscular blond man walks out. He's very handsome. He's covered in tattoos and looks good even though he's dressed in jeans and a god-awful bowl-ing shirt with a white top underneath. I wonder if this is his usual look.

Even with the shirt, he screams bad boy.

The bright pattern isn't fooling anybody.

Blue eyes lock on me. "Bronte Pierce?"

"That's me," I say, shaking his hand as he offers it. "Nice to meet you."

"I'm Crow, and I'm in charge here. We have two mechanics coming in and out to help Cam put to-gether the bikes. But it's a small group since we only do custom pieces."

So this *is* who messaged me yesterday.

"So are you Abbie's partner?" I ask, since Uncle Neville said he owned the place. If he is, she has done very, very well for herself.

He gives me a confused look, then laughs. I don't want to admit what the sound of his laugh does to me; it's deep and all consuming. Great, now I'm having weird feelings about my cousin's partner and I haven't even met my cousin yet. Way to build a relationship. Oh yeah, and he's my boss.

Snap out of it, Bronte. You're here to work, and that's it.

Once he's done laughing, he still has a smirk on his face. I'm not going to lie; it kind of annoys me. "No, Temper is Abbie's partner. Don't let him hear you ask me that."

"But you said you're in charge. I was told Abbie's partner owns the place."

His smirk is gone and now he just looks annoyed.

"Yes, Temper technically owns it, but I am in charge here. Is that going to be a problem?"

Shit. Great, first I was attracted to the boss, and now I'm pissing him off. "Nope. Not a problem. Sorry, I just found out about Abbie, so I'm playing catch-up. You're in charge. Got it."

And apparently not a topic I will bring up again.

He looks at me skeptically but gives me a brief nod. "We basically need someone to man the reception, answer phones, order parts and stay on top of all the bookkeeping. Sound manageable?"

I decide that honesty is the best policy. "I have done some admin work before, but I don't know anything about bikes or ordering parts. But I'm a quick learner and I'm sure I can pick it up." I give him my best I-am-confident look.

I hope he buys it.

It's the truth, though. I've done work more complicated than this, and I'm eager to learn and be the best at whatever job I am doing. I'm someone who takes pride in her work, and I know that I'm going to be an asset to his team.

"Abbie said you were a private investigator?"

"I was an assistant to one, yes." I nod.

"Huh. I would have guessed a librarian," he comments, making my eyes widen. I mean, I was only just thinking the same thing based on how I dressed today, but it's rude of him to mention that, especially after only just meeting me. "I hope you're able to handle the job, and don't expect any special treatment just because you're Abbie's long-lost cousin."

My jaw drops. His comment really gets to me, even though I don't want to let him see that. "I don't expect any special treatment."

"That's good, but not true, because special treatment got you this job in the first place," he replies casually, as if his words aren't hitting every damn nerve.

I should have known that this job was going to come with a catch, and it looks like I've found it. An annoying, smart-ass boss.

"I might have gotten this job because of my family, but that doesn't mean I'm not a hard worker who's going to be an asset to your business," I fire back, eyes narrowing. "But I guess only time will prove that to you, especially since you seem to already have made your mind up about me."

He studies me for a moment, giving nothing away with his expression. "Look, I take this job seriously and I need someone who will also take it seriously, regardless of who your family is or what you used to do."

"Understood."

"I guess time *will* tell. Come on, I'll show you around." He opens a door behind the main reception desk. "So back here is the staff room. There's a kitchen, a bathroom and lots and lots of parts back there. There's also a bed because Dee thought it needed one for when he's here and wants to take a nap."

I have no idea who Dee is, but I nod. "I can assure you that I won't be napping on the job," I promise.

He doesn't reply. After the brief tour, he shows me

the computer I'll be using and the software I need to learn to keep stock of all the motorcycle parts. It's pretty straightforward, and for the first time since I found out I was going to be working here, I feel a little more confident.

"I'm going to leave a list of contact numbers here. You should have mine from yesterday, but it's the first one," he says.

"Okay."

Then he gets up, removes his bowling shirt, revealing biceps to die for, picks up a leather vest off the chair and puts it on. I can't seem to take my eyes off him, which annoys me, because I need to control myself. But him in that leather vest, white tank top underneath, his beautiful tattoos covering his muscular arms…it really works for him. He even flicks his blond hair back, just like he's in some fucking advertisement or something.

"You're a biker," I say out loud.

He tilts his head to the side and gives me a look like he thinks I'm stupid. "They really didn't give you much information at all, did they? Are you sure this is the place you want to work?"

As he turns, I see the words Knights of Fury MC written on the back of his vest.

I'm working for a biker gang?

Just what crowd exactly does my new cousin hang with?

"Yes. I was just surprised, that's all," I say as I watch him head toward the door.

I start to panic. I may feel a little confident, but

I'm not ready to be left alone. What if customers call? Or come in?

"Wait, you're going?" I call after him.

"Yep," he calls back, sounding unimpressed, and walks over to a big, badass black motorcycle. I stand at the entrance, watching him, wondering how the hell he can leave me alone here with nothing more than a crash course on how to work here.

"You can't leave. I have no idea what I'm supposed to do."

He kick-starts his motorcycle, the engine loud. "I thought you were a fast learner. Was that a lie?"

Well, shit. He has me there—I did say that. But I am not in the wrong here. "But what if a customer calls? And besides 'admin work' you didn't really tell me what I should start with."

"I think you'll be able to figure it out. I have somewhere to be." And with that, he starts driving off.

Fuck.

As the sound of his rumbling engine disappears, I sit down at my desk and drum my fingers on the table. A few seconds later, the phone rings.

Shit.

I've always prided myself on being competent and adaptable, and it looks like I'm going to have to prove that right now.

"Hello, Fast & Fury Custom Motorcycles, Bronte speaking." I try to hide the indecision in my voice.

"Bronte, it's me, Abbie. I just thought I'd call in and say hi."

Relief washes over me. "Hey, Abbie. It is so great

to officially meet you. Or rather talk to you. I want to thank you for getting me this job. It came at the perfect time and I'm indebted to you."

"It isn't a problem. I'm just getting used to having a father, and now to hear I have an uncle and a cousin. I'm thrilled! And family looks out for each other."

I laugh. "Well, you haven't met us yet; don't get too excited."

"So how are you doing on your first day?"

"Crow just left me here alone, so I'm not sure how my first day is going."

She laughs softly. "Do you want me to come in? I'll bring you lunch. I've been waiting to meet you, Bronte. The second I found out I had a cousin my age, I was so excited."

"Me too," I admit. "I'd love for you to come in, but only if you don't mind."

"I'll be there in an hour," she replies.

When we hang up, I feel so much better. I can't believe what an asshole Crow is, leaving me here alone on my first day, but Abbie has saved the day for me.

And I'm not going to let him win.

Before Abbie arrives, I do what work I can, which includes organizing all the paperwork on my desk, which happens to be a big pile, and going through the parts-order sheets and trying to understand the system they use here. I pick up on some inconsistencies and a few mistakes, which I fix and make note of.

It's surprisingly a lot of work. They really did need someone in this role, because their documents aren't filed or organized. It must be hard to figure out what the hell is going on here.

Crow might not know it yet, but he does need me here, and I'm going to prove that to him.

Chapter Three

"It's so weird that you know my dad more than I do," Abbie says, and pops a fry in her mouth. She's absolutely beautiful, with Uncle Neville's amber eyes, long dark hair like mine and a curvaceous figure. "I mean, we've started seeing each other a lot more now, but it's still like learning someone from scratch, you know?"

"I love Uncle Neville. He's a little guarded, but I'd like to say we're as close as he lets me be," I say, pick up the soda she brought me and take a sip. "He would always be there for any of us without hesitation."

Abbie laughs. "That totally sounds like him!"

"I was so surprised to find out he had a daughter he didn't know about. I'm still trying to process the whole thing. It almost sounds like it could be a movie."

"You and me both," she says. "The whole situation has been drama-filled and full of surprises. It's been really complicated too."

"Complicated how?"

"Just all the stuff with Dad and who he is. My

mom has not been excited that not only am I living here, but I'm also spending time with him. It's been a whirlwind, but I'm pretty happy where I'm at now. I grew up without a father, so it's nice having him now. Better late than never."

I don't know what she's referring to about Uncle Neville, but I don't press. I guess the whole thing would have been so hard to deal with, for everyone involved.

"I'm just glad that we all get to know you now," I say, smiling.

"Me too." She beams. "I mean, it sucks we didn't get to grow up together, but you know what? I feel strangely comfortable with you already."

"I feel the same," I admit. "I feel like I've known you for longer than just an hour, that's for sure."

It sounds cliché, but it's true. This girl was just meant to be in my life, I know it. Blood connections can be strong.

"Uncle Neville never told me that this place was owned by a motorcycle club."

"It is. Are you familiar with motorcycle clubs?" she asks, watching my reaction.

I shake my head no.

"When I was growing up, they came into my family's bar, so I had an idea of them, but I didn't really know what they did."

"So how did you end up part of it?" I ask.

Abbie smiles. "It's a long story and I don't want to scare you. My story with the Knights is definitely…"

She pauses, trying to come up with the right word. "…unconventional."

Now I'm curious. "You have to tell me more." Unconventional could mean a lot of things, and I really want to hear this story.

"Let's just say it started with a kidnapping but ended with me getting a happily ever after," she explains, wincing.

My eyes feel like they are going to bulge out of my head.

"I know it sounds crazy, and if I'm being honest, it *is* crazy. But I fell in love with the man, and he's so good to me. It all worked out in the end."

I don't know what to say, so I stay silent.

"And now I've scared you. I told you, it's not a story for the fainthearted. But about Fast & Fury—it's a completely legitimate business, so you have nothing to worry about," she assures me, reaching out and touching my arm. "You can trust the men here. Temper is my fiancé, so you can most definitely trust him. He knows you are my family, and that means something here."

"Right. Crow mentioned that you were with a man named Temper," I say, trying to put the word *kidnapping* out of my head. "Uncle Neville mentioned your partner owned this place, but I didn't know he was your fiancé. Congratulations. Also, what's with the names around here?"

"Thank you." She beams, and then laughs. "Bikers and their road names, or nicknames. You'll get used to them. Temper and I, we're quite an unlikely couple, but he is definitely the man I'm meant to be with. He used to come into the bar I worked at, one my family owns, every single year. He used to ask me out each time, and each time I'd say no."

"Why?" I ask, smiling at her love story.

"Because I knew my life was going to change if I said yes," she admits, ducking her head. "And I was never ready. And when I was, I said yes."

"That's a beautiful story," I say. "Do I want to know why they call him Temper?"

"Probably not." She grins.

I shake my head at her. "You're crazy, but I like you."

And I mean that. This whole thing is madness, yet somehow I'm enjoying meeting new people, and seeing and hearing about the lives they lead.

She laughs. "All the couples in the MC have their own story. Skylar and Saint have known each other since Sky was a kid and had a crush on him. Renny and Izzy got drunk and married in Vegas before they even knew they liked each other. Skylar said that she knows you."

I nod. "Yeah, I love Skylar, but we haven't spoken in a bit. I had no idea she was tied to the MC, either."

What a small world.

"And that sounds like stories that I need to hear in detail," I add.

Abbie's and Skylar's stories seem to have worked out, but I can't imagine how dangerous being with bikers is. I mean, kidnapping?

The office phone rings, and Abbie quickly answers

it, but I soon realize she has about as much idea as me on what's going on.

"Sure, we can custom a bike for you. Could you come into the shop?" She pauses. "Not today, maybe tomorrow? Great, thanks." She turns to me. "Hopefully Cam is in tomorrow. This is my first time even answering a phone in here, so I have no idea what's going on."

"I really hope so," I reply. "Don't worry, I have no idea what's going on either, and I actually work here."

We both laugh, just as Crow walks back in. I can imagine how we look. Abbie is sitting on the desk while I'm on the seat, both of us surrounded by food and drinks, laughing like we're having a good old time. This isn't the impression I wanted to give him, considering our interaction this morning, and even though Abbie is here, I know he's going to be judging the hell out of me. I don't know why it seems like he's looking for a reason to dislike me, but it sure does feel that way.

"Working hard, I see," he murmurs.

And there we have it.

"She's on her lunch break," Abbie speaks up, grinning, unaware of the tension between us. "I brought you some food, too. Oh, and someone is coming in tomorrow to design their bike."

"Cameron will be back in tomorrow," he says, sitting down on the desk next to her. "She's finally back from vacation and can handle that. Does Temper know you're here?"

"Nope," she replies nonchalantly, leaning back on

her palms. "He's out on club business, and I'm sure he'll be happy that I'll be hanging around more, since my beautiful cousin is employed here. You'll definitely be seeing more of me."

He looks between the two of us and mutters something about trouble. He and Abbie are clearly friends, and he doesn't look at her with the same disdain he does me. I have no idea what I've done to get this reaction from him, but I pretend I don't notice.

Abbie stays for another half hour and then heads home, leaving me alone with Crow once more. I miss her the second that she's gone—the vibe in the workplace changes instantly. I don't know what he has against me, but I know one thing for sure: I'm going to prove him wrong.

I'm unsure if he does this to all new employees or if it's just me, but I'm not going to let him in.

He's met his match.

"You made me start today knowing that I'd be here alone, didn't you?" I ask, lifting my chin. "Let me guess, there's probably a camera in here somewhere too."

He was testing me. Maybe he wanted to see if I was capable, but more likely I think he wanted to see if he could trust me. Abbie's arrival would have ruined the whole thing, though, and now that she knows I'm hired, he can't exactly go back on his word.

He says nothing.

"Am I wrong?" I press, watching him as he glances at his phone, all but ignoring me.

"We can't just let anyone work here; we need to

be able to trust you. You'd be surprised by the shit we've seen employees do the second they think no one is watching."

"And I thought I had trust issues. Well, I'm sure you'll be happy to know that I just saved the company thousands and thousands of dollars," I say, trying to hide my smugness and failing.

"What are you talking about?" he asks, sounding like he doesn't believe me for a second.

I'm happier than I should be, passing on the next bit of information to him. But he deserves this after all the shit he's given me, and for assuming that I was going to do something wrong today.

I didn't.

I raise a piece of paper. "I was looking at the parts list that you are ordering, and someone was about to accidentally order sixteen of the sixteen-inch ape hangers instead of the one that was required."

He walks over and takes the document from me, eying it and then glancing at me. "Fucking hell."

"You're welcome," I say, sounding overly chirpy. "I've just saved your business over fifteen thousand dollars."

He clears his throat. "Okay then."

Okay then? That's all I get? No thank-you, nothing?

"This is the weirdest first day at a job, ever," I say to myself, turning my attention back to the computer screen.

"I'd think this would be boring compared to working for a private investigator," he adds, having to get the last word. Is he going to be here every day?

"Is there anything else you'd like me to do?" I ask, changing the subject. "I saw the folder full of receipts—I can file them for you and add it to the online system."

"That sounds good." He pauses and then adds, "And perhaps you could check over the rest of the orders to make sure no one else made any mistakes."

Ha.

For the next hour I do just that, double-checking someone else's work. Then Crow tells me I can go home early, and he'll see me tomorrow.

I don't know if I'm looking forward to it or dreading it.

Nadia calls me as soon as I get into my car, asking if I want to come to her place for dinner so she can hear about my first day at work. Considering I had no plans for dinner and was just going to make some two-minute noodles, her offer sounds perfect. Since we don't see each other at work anymore, we both need to put in the effort to stay in contact, and I appreciate that she's doing it.

"Hey," I say, smiling as I give her a hug after she opens her apartment door. "How are you?"

"I'm good. How's your new job?" she asks as we step inside. Her apartment is small, but open and modern, with white walls and gray furniture.

"It was…interesting," I say, sitting down on her

couch and placing my bag next to me. "I don't even know where to start."

"This sounds juicy."

"So my cousin got me the job," I say. "A cousin I didn't know that I had until recently."

"What?" she asks, confusion on her face.

I give her the rundown on my uncle and Abbie, and then tell her how my day went.

"So basically your boss is a hottie slash asshole," she concludes, eyes going wide. "And you're working with motorcycle parts, something you have no idea about."

"Yeah, pretty much."

"I'm still trying to process the whole new cousin thing," she admits, shaking her head at me. "Never a dull day with you, is it?"

"Only as of recent," I say, sighing.

We move to the dining table and she serves dinner—pasta, garlic bread and red wine.

"Thanks for inviting me over," I say.

"No problem. I do feel really bad about having to let you go, so I hope the new job is amazing, Bronte," she says.

"You have no reason to feel bad," I assure her. "I am not upset at you at all, okay? So don't even worry about it."

She smiles sadly. "It's just a shit feeling, you know? You're one of my closest friends and I loved working with you. Work isn't the same without you. I had a stakeout yesterday, and it was so boring waiting there in my car alone."

I grin. "It's just how it has to be for now, but it's nice to know that I'm missed."

"You really are."

"We will still be close and see each other all the time," I say. "Okay?"

"Okay." She nods. "Thank you for not holding a grudge."

"You didn't have a choice, Nadia," I tell her. "Don't worry about me, I'll be fine. I *am* fine. Hopefully business will pick up, and without you having to pay an extra employee, you can now make more of a profit."

"I hope so too," she admits. "If I have to close the doors, I don't know what I'm going to do. Maybe they'll hire me with you at the garage."

I laugh. "That can be plan B. Plan A is trying to keep the business going and thriving."

"Agreed. I feel a little better now that I know you have some eye candy at your new work," she says, laughing.

I shake my head at her. "It would be a lot better if he didn't talk."

"We'll see," she murmurs. "I don't think I've seen you let a guy get to you like this one has."

I puff out a breath. "Yeah, you're right. I need to not let him do that."

If only it were that easy.

We finish our meal, and I help her clean up and then head home.

Tomorrow it will be time to do it all over again.

* * *

"I'm Cameron," the most beautiful tattooed blonde says as soon as I step into work the next morning. She looks like a mixture of badass and Barbie, her denim shorts showing off her long legs, her pink top fringed and frayed. I find myself liking her instantly. "Everyone calls me Cam. It's nice to meet you, Bronte. Abbie called me last night and told me all about you."

So this is Cam.

"News travels fast around here," I muse, smirking.

"You have no idea. I'm one of the mechanics, and I also do most of the designing and am the creative and artistic manager," she explains, walking with me to my desk. "I gave myself that title but now everyone rolls with it. I work here full time too, so we'll be seeing a lot of each other."

"You tell me what you need, and I'll handle it," I tell her, turning the computer on. "Crow gave me the rundown, but I'm still not exactly sure what I'm supposed to be getting done every day."

"You're basically the glue that holds this place together." She grins, flashing straight white teeth. Her beautiful green eyes dash to the phone as it rings. "And it begins. Anything you don't know how to answer, put them on hold and call out to me."

The man on the phone is asking me when we can fit him in to fix his Harley when Crow walks in, the whole atmosphere in the warehouse instantly changing with each stomp of his black biker boots. Cameron instantly goes over to greet him, and the two of them embrace, leaving my stomach in knots.

Don't be ridiculous, I tell myself. I can't stand the guy and barely know him. So why do I feel jealous that she gets sunshine and rainbows and I get moody?

"Look how tanned you've gotten," I hear him say. "Tell me everything about your vacation."

I can't even remember what I say to the man on the phone, but we hang up and my attention is solely on Crow and Cameron. I don't think they're a couple, or he'd have known how her trip was already. And who cares if they are? He's an asshole and it's none of my business what he does.

Crow comes over, and I notice he has a bandage wrapped around his knuckles on his right hand. I wonder what he did to himself.

"Boxing at the clubhouse," he says, eyes on me.

"Oh, I…" I trail off, not knowing how to reply to him answering a question I only asked in my head.

Boxing at the…clubhouse?

Clearing my throat, I lean back in my chair and study him. Crow's enthusiastic attitude when he saw Cameron is long gone, a broodiness he seems to only reserve for me left in its place.

What's his deal with me?

The phone rings, saving me. "I guess I better get back to work." Saved by the bell.

"Fast & Fury, Bronte speaking," I say, ignoring his blue eyes on me. I schedule an appointment for the client to come in, and only when I hang up does he speak.

"Your hair looks…different today." He walks away, leaving my eyes narrowed.

He doesn't give away whether that's a good thing or not, which annoys me.

He annoys me.

Cameron walks up, brow furrowed. She turns, tilting her head to the side and studying me. "Crow is the most laid-back, funny guy I've ever met in my life. I don't know why he's so weird around you."

"I must have that effect on people," I reply in a dry tone, still staring at his back. I don't know what's up with him, but his energy is all over the place, and he clearly has a chip on his shoulder when it comes to me. I know I only have to put up with him at work, and he's not terrible to be around, but he just leaves me feeling a little…off-kilter.

And I don't like it.

"He's a good-looking man," she continues, sitting down on the edge of the wooden desk and crossing her legs. "You'd be surprised how many times women come in here pretending they are looking at motorcycles to try to get his or one of the other men's attention. It's sad, really."

I don't want to ask her the next question, but my curiosity wins out. "The two of you have never…"

"Me and Crow?" she asks, eyes going wide as she shakes her head. "No. He's like a brother to me. He took a huge chance on me, giving me this job, and I'll never forget that. There aren't many places that want to hire someone who has done time, let alone a woman in a place like this, but the Knights don't judge."

Wait, what?

Cameron has been to prison?

She leans down closer and adds, "It's too bad I have zero attraction to him. He's hot. Tall, too. Far over six feet, none of that 'five-eleven, almost six foot in shoes' bullshit I get when I'm online dating."

I burst out laughing, earning a dirty look from the man in question. "Shame he's an asshole."

"The hot ones usually are," she murmurs. I want to ask her about the prison thing, but I figure if she wants me to know, she will tell me.

Abbie drops in on her lunch break with her fiancé, Temper. I'm not going to lie, the man looks a little scary with his huge build and dark eyes, but he shakes my hand and welcomes me to the Fast & Fury family.

"Abbie has been talking about you nonstop," he adds, glancing down at her lovingly. "It's nice to finally meet you."

"It's nice to meet you too."

"I have to head out back to do a few things before we leave, so if you both will excuse me."

"Okay," Abbie says, turning to me with a big smile on her face. "How's it been? I wanted to text you and realized I didn't have your number, so I thought I'd drop in and get it." She holds out her phone and types in the numbers as I say them.

"It's been really good," I say, eyes darting to Crow to see what he's up to. He's currently talking to a customer. "Everyone has been really welcoming."

Besides Crow, of course.

"That's good to hear. I thought they would be. I

know not many work here, but I don't think you could find a better crew of people."

"So far so good," I agree with her.

"So I was thinking, if you don't have any plans this weekend, do you want to do something? My friends are dying to meet you, and Skylar of course wants to see you. I'd love to spend some time together," she says, pushing her hair back behind her ear.

"That sounds really nice," I reply.

How could I not when she is so genuine? I don't think many people could say no to the woman in front of me.

"Perfect." She grins.

Crow wanders over and casually wraps his arm around her. "What happened to you last night?"

"I had to finish my assignment," she explains, crossing her arms over her chest. "So I locked myself away until it was over. Pretty hard considering how loud you all are."

Do they all live together? The two of them are obviously very comfortable with each other, something I can tell from their body language. Abbie must be close friends with most of the members in the MC, especially considering Temper is the president. Does that make her a queen of the MC of sorts?

"We tried to keep it down," he says, removing his arm and fondly nudging her. "Until Saint started pouring shots. It all went downhill from there."

"I don't know how you can function the next morning." Abbie smirks, rolling her eyes. "I'd be suffering in bed with a hangover, yet all of you were up earlier than me and ready to start the day."

"Our bodies have adapted," he jokes, turning to me as if only just remembering that I'm standing here. "What about you, Bronte? You much of a drinker?"

I shake my head. "No, not really." Which is the truth.

"What's your vice then?" he presses, studying me. I don't miss the look Abbie gives him. It clearly says *leave her alone* but he simply ignores her.

"What's yours?" I fire back, arching my brow. "Just drinking? Or do you have more than one?"

I bet women is one of them. Lots of them.

"I'm the one asking the questions here," he states, crossing his arms and narrowing his blue eyes.

"Crow," Abbie interrupts, scowling at him. "She doesn't have to tell you shit about her personal life. Maybe if you want to know more about her, you should have a normal conversation with her instead of all this weird posturing that's going on."

"I'm not allowed to make conversation?" he asks, her comment now the big elephant in the room. "I'm just trying to get to know our new employee."

Abbie's about to reply when I decide to answer his damn question, just to prove that he doesn't intimidate me.

Not one bit.

"I think shopping is probably my vice," I reply, shrugging. "Even that I'm always in control of, but I do enjoy it a little too much. But as long as I'm paying for it and maintaining myself, I don't think it's a problem. Alcohol, drugs and smoking don't appeal to me, but I'm not judging people who do what they have to do to fight their demons."

I don't know how the hell this talk turned deep, but here we are.

"Anyway, I better get back to work. Abbie, text me the details and I'll see you on the weekend," I say, smiling warmly, ignoring Crow and leaving my desk to see what Cameron is up to. The guy makes me want to leave my own damn workspace.

Gritting my teeth, I vow to myself: I'm not going to let a man that goes by the name of a damn bird get one over on me.

Chapter Four

"Holy shit, you designed this?" I ask Cameron, eying the motorcycle that now looks like a piece of artwork. Red flames come off the matte black in a 3D effect, fading into orange and yellow.

"I did the design, the artwork, everything." She beams, circling the bike and admiring it. "Dee, one of the Knights, gave me free rein to do whatever I wanted. I think he's going to love it."

"I think so, too. Man, you are so talented. I bet all of the Knights come in here to get their bikes done." I don't even ride, and suddenly I want a custom bike.

"Yeah, they do. I think it started out as just a place for them to custom their own bikes, but it grew. It's now known as the best custom bike shop in the city," she explains, pride in her tone. "We have a waiting list for people wanting a one-of-a-kind, custom bike. And we're a small shop, so we take our time creating them, which makes them even more exclusive. I do the designs and then we have the mechanics that work in the garage."

"I feel like I need to do a little research so I actually know what I'm talking about when customers ask me," I say, opening the lid from the lunch I packed from home and eating one of the nuts from the top of my salad. Not long after Abbie left, so did Crow, and I have to admit the workplace is much less stressful with him gone. I can now enjoy my lunch break talking shit with Cam without the tension Crow brings.

"I'll help you and guide you through everything. You'll be a pro in no time," she assures me. "My mom said she's going to drop in and see me today, so if you see someone who looks like me but older and with pink hair, let me know."

"Will do," I say, grinning at the image. "You're lucky to have your mom around."

"You don't?" she asks, lifting her head and looking at me.

"No, she died when I was a kid," I say, staring into my salad. "She had cancer. She and my dad had an epic love story. He's never loved anyone again, never even introduced a woman to me. I wonder if I'll ever find that type of love, or if it even exists anymore."

Cancer. The disease that took my mother may just be my downfall, too.

Or maybe it will just take away my chance to give life.

"I'm sorry about your mom," she says, pulling up a crate and sitting next to me. "That type of love does exist—I see it every day. Temper and Abbie, they have that. Sky and Saint. Renny and Izzy. It's out there. I don't know if *I'm* ever going to find it, but it's out there."

"So you have hope for others but not for you?" I ask, frowning. "Have you seen yourself? I'm surprised you don't have men coming in lining up to see you."

"I'd like a line to form," she jokes, laughing. "Men and women, I'm not fussed—I like them both."

We laugh together at that, and I like how open she is about everything. Cam hides nothing—she is who she is, and I appreciate that about her.

"What type of women are you into?" I ask. "Do they need to be over six feet, too?"

A man I've never seen before walks in, eying the two of us. "Hey, Cam." He looks at me and grins. "Bronte?"

I nod.

"Damn, Crow never mentioned how cute you are," he says, openly checking me out.

Of course Crow didn't.

"I'm Dee." He offers me his hand and I shake it.

"Nice to meet you, Dee. You come to see your piece of art?"

He rubs his hands together. "I have, and damn, she is looking good. Cam, you've outdone yourself."

The two of them coo over the bike while I head back out front, and sit back down at my desk. I've only just opened a tab on Internet Explorer when Crow walks back in, holding a big-ass bouquet of flowers.

"Who are those for?" I ask before I'm able to stop myself.

He places them on my table and leans forward on

his palms. I can smell his cologne, a wild, woodsy scent, and I have to stop myself from wanting to just melt into him.

"Cam," he says quietly, blue eyes raking over my face. "It's her birthday tomorrow, but I won't be in, so I wanted to surprise her."

"Oh. She's in the back with Dee," I reply, licking my suddenly dry lips. "Who, by the way, was surprised that you didn't tell him I was cute."

Crap, I shouldn't have said that. It's a bit unprofessional, but I wanted to get a rise out of him. Besides, I enjoy putting him on the spot, but I should have known that nothing ever fazes Crow.

"I'm not a woman. I don't sit around gossiping and discussing other people." He tilts his head a little. "Why? You want to hear that I'm going around saying that the new chick at the garage is a hottie?"

"Just repeating what he said, and don't act like men don't gossip," I reply with a smirk, glancing back at the flowers. "They are beautiful. I had no idea it's Cam's birthday tomorrow. I'll have to bring in a cake or something." Everyone has a few talents in their life, and one of mine happens to be cake decorating.

"Yeah, she doesn't like to make a fuss, so of course we do that for her. By the way, good work with the parts order you put in this morning. You have a good eye."

"Thanks."

He picks up the flowers and takes them out back to give them to her, and I can hear her yelling in happiness when she sees them.

It was a thoughtful thing for him to do.

Maybe Crow's not so bad after all.

The next day my dad drops into work unexpectedly, food in his hands.

"Hey, Dad, what are you doing here?" I ask, giving him a big hug.

"I was in the neighborhood, so I thought I'd drop in and see how you're doing," he explains as he glances around the warehouse. "Pretty cool place. I brought you your favorite burger and fries."

"Thanks, Dad," I say, smiling at him. He always did things like this when I was working with Nadia. It's what I love about him—he is so thoughtful.

Crow walks back out and sees us standing there, and quickly comes over.

"Dad, this is my boss, Crow. Crow, this is my dad," I introduce.

Crow offers Dad his hand. "Nice to meet you, sir."

"And you," Dad replies, glancing over to me. "I hope you don't mind, just wanted to check out Bronte's new workplace and see how she's doing."

"Not at all," Crow replies, eyes going to me. "She's a great worker, we're lucky to have her."

Well, that's news to me. I can't look away from Crow as he says kind words about me to my dad, who appears extremely proud. In fact, his smile is wider than I've seen it in a long time. I'm happy, because I know how proud he was of me at my old job, so it's nice to know that hasn't changed with this one.

And Crow? I think for the first time I can see what

everyone else says about him. He can be charming. Friendly. And yeah, he's cute.

Dangerously so.

"She's a great girl."

"That she is," Crow replies. "Do you want a tour of the warehouse? I can show you…"

He leads my dad away, like he came here to visit him instead of me, and shows him all of the fancy motorcycles, the two of them suddenly best friends.

I eat my burger and fries.

Alone.

Once the tour is done, Dad returns to me. "This place is pretty awesome."

"It is, isn't it?" I reply, smiling at him. "Thanks for the food, Dad. And for dropping by. It's definitely made my day. Even if you've spent more time with Crow than you have with me."

Dad just laughs. "I like him, he's a good man."

Is this my dad giving his approval for Crow? He's my boss! I want to tell him that is not happening, but I don't want anyone to overhear that conversation, so it's going to have to wait for another time.

"He's okay, I suppose," I admit.

Sometimes.

"He promised me he'd look after you," he adds, winking at me. "I better get going—Neville and I have some business to work out."

"Nothing serious?" I ask, remembering their intense conversation at the barbecue.

Dad looks at me in surprise. "You worry too much. You know Neville, always has a scheme. We just have to discuss some things then we're going to see a movie."

It's so cute that the two of them go on little brother dates, and make sure to spend time with each other as much as they can. They both have such an amazing bond.

"Okay, Dad," I say, giving him a big, tight hug. "I love you."

"I love you too, princess."

Locking my apartment door behind me, I stretch my neck from side to side to release some of the tension. After placing the grocery bags on the kitchen counter, I pull out my phone and slump down on the stool at the bench. It's been a long week, and I'm glad it's finally the weekend.

My phone is pretty dry, apart from messages from my dad and Billie, one of my closest friends. What are you doing tonight? she asks.

Billie is the type of friend where we won't speak for a few weeks at a time, lost in work, life and relationships, but our friendship is always as strong as ever. I know if I need her she will be here in a heartbeat, and vice versa.

Netflix and chilling, I type back.

Alone, I also add.

She replies instantly. Get dressed. I'll be there in an hour.

I type out a few different messages, all stating that there's no way in hell I'm leaving my apartment tonight, but hey, maybe time catching up with Billie is exactly what the doctor ordered.

I've showered and thrown on some black, ripped skinny jeans with a lace bodysuit underneath when I hear her knocking. She always does the exact same knock, two slow taps followed by three quick ones. I don't know if she realizes she does it.

"Hello," I greet her with a wide smile. "You look beautiful."

Her red hair has grown down her back, similar to mine, and it suits her. She's wearing a white dress, her green eyes lined and smudged in black eye shadow. Growing up, people always thought we were sisters and we milked it for all it was worth. Now, though, she's always changing her look and I couldn't keep up with her even if I wanted to.

I met Billie in kindergarten. Apparently I gave her a once-over and she thought I was a snob. But there was this really mean kid in class—I don't even re- member her name—and we bonded over our mutual dislike of her. The rest is history.

"I needed a change," she says, touching her locks.

Closing the door, I take a wild guess. "New hair means you're single, doesn't it? What happened to Troy?"

"Troy who?" she asks, dismissing her boyfriend of three years. "He's old news. How have you been? How's the new job going? You need to fill me in on all that, because a simple 'I have a new job' text mes- sage isn't going to cut it." She lifts up the champagne bottle she brought with her. "Let me pour us a glass, and then you can update me on your life."

I get comfy on the couch as she brings two glasses with her and fills them to the brim. After catching her up on me losing my job, finding a new one, finding out about Abbie, and all things Crow, she sits there with her mouth open.

"Your life is way more interesting than mine," she finally says, after a big swallow. "I'm glad your work situation sorted itself out. I know how stressful that must have been for a control freak like you."

"Not going to lie, it was definitely stressful. Now what happened with Troy? Last I heard the two of you were planning to get engaged soon."

She swirls the liquid in her glass, eyes hypnotized. "I had a bad feeling, so I checked his phone. I know, I know," she murmurs, looking up at me. "I know I shouldn't have, but I needed to know. And I was right; he'd been cheating on me. You should always trust your gut."

"I'm sorry," I say, fingers tightening around my glass. "What an asshole! He was punching way above his weight with you, and then he has the nerve to cheat on you?"

"That's exactly what I said to him," she grits out, teeth clenched. She waves her hand. "Anyway, it's done now. I kicked him out, he's Veronica's problem now. I'm glad I found out the truth. Imagine if I'd married the scumbag?"

"So true," I agree, then mutter under my breath,

"He better hope I don't catch him down an alleyway or something."

Billie laughs and finishes the rest of her drink. "You know me, I'll be fine. I mean, it hurts, but he obviously wasn't for me, so. There's no point crying over dick that wasn't that great anyway."

I pour us more champagne, and we toast to that. "So what do you want to do tonight? Dinner?"

"Dinner sounds perfect."

Although I've known Billie for a long time, and I know that her "dinner" always ends up being café Patrón shots, dancing on stage, and potentially throwing up on the cab ride home.

I wish I were joking.

She can be a mess, but she's my mess, especially now that Troy is toast.

"I'll call a cab," I state, grabbing my handbag and making sure it has all the essentials to survive a night out with single Billie.

"And I'll finish this champagne." She smiles, doing a little dance, shaking her hips.

Shit.

Here's to me surviving tonight.

Chapter Five

"Dude, you have to taste this, it's amazing," Billie says, bringing the chopsticks to my lips.

I take a bite and have to agree. "Okay, we need to order more of that. Plus, filling your stomach is a good idea."

"Filling *our* stomachs," she replies, and eats another dumpling. "When's the last time you got drunk with me?"

I rack my brain. "Your last birthday?"

"You had two drinks," she reminds me, lifting her brows and chewing slowly. "And then you left early to finish some work. I think you were investigating some guy that was cheating on his wife. Oh my God, why didn't I just ask you to look into Troy? We could have found out about him much earlier."

"Because you trusted him and thought he was someone that he wasn't?"

"Yeah, what a rookie mistake that was," she grumbles, pursing her red lips. "I swear, I'm going to stay single for the rest of my life. I'm destined to be a spinster. I don't need kids. I'll just be a cool auntie to all yours when you have them."

Her comment hurts me more than she will ever know, but then again, it's my fault for not telling her there's a chance that I might never have kids.

"What about sex?" I ask, changing the subject. "And don't you even try to tell me you don't need that."

"Sex isn't a problem for me. Sex is easy. I'll find a fuck buddy or two, or a friend with benefits, that's easily solved," she replies, shrugging. "Worse comes to worst, all my friends keep talking about some sex toy that's supposed to even be better than the real thing."

I laugh at her problem-solving skills. "Not all men are like Troy. I'm sure one day you'll meet someone worthy of you, and then I'll get to be the cool auntie."

"Maybe you and Crow will have a nest of little baby Crows."

I roll my eyes at her. "This little intervention tonight isn't about me, it's about you."

"Yeah, but you have a love interest. All I have right now is bitterness," she says, and eats the last of the food from her plate. "And perhaps tomorrow, alcohol poisoning."

"It's been a while since I've danced," I admit. We decided to sit outside of the restaurant, and I find myself enjoying the hustle and bustle, the music, the lights, and the people. "It's a beautiful night. Thanks for dragging me out. I would have been on the couch in my pajamas with a tub of ice cream otherwise."

"Thanks for coming out with me," she says, lifting her glass. "You are the one person who knows me in all of my stages: the old me, the present me, and the new me. You know I love you, right?"

"I love you too. To the present versions of us."

We clink our glasses together, finish up, and then head to our next spot for the night.

A bar.

Stepping inside, I kind of wish I'd dressed up a little more. I barely put on any makeup other than some mascara and highlighter, my hair wild down my back. Billie's obviously a little more prepared, fitting in perfectly in her dress and heels.

"Have you been here before?" I ask, leaning on the glass bar and waiting to be served.

"Nope," she replies, looking at the dance floor. "I think it's new, that's why it's so busy. Pretty cool, though, huh?"

"Yeah," I have to admit. It's playing the type of music I love, R&B and reggae, and my hips move to the beat of their own accord. "What's it called again?"

"Kamikaze," a familiar voice answers from behind me. My head snaps back so fast I'm surprised it doesn't break.

What are the chances I'd run into his ass tonight?

"Crow," I say, ducking my head.

Billie looks over my shoulder, eying him. "Hello."

Sighing, I say, "This is Billie. Billie, this is Crow."

I hate when people don't introduce other people. I find it extremely rude, so I make sure I get that out of the way immediately.

"Nice to meet you," Crow says to her politely, then brings those ocean-blue eyes back to me. "I thought you weren't much of a drinker."

"I'm not," I reply, lifting my chin and narrowing my eyes. "That doesn't mean that I never have a drink. This your new hunting ground?"

His lip twitches. "Something like that. We actually just opened this place."

"What don't you own?" I grumble, scanning the place in a new light. The Knights must make a shitload of money, because it seems like they have their fingers in all kinds of pies.

"She doesn't drink," Billie pipes in, smirking. "Or leave the house. I had to drag her ass out tonight."

Crow grins and signals the bartender. "Tough week at work, Bronte?"

"Something like that," I mutter, checking him out in his black shirt and jeans. "Run out of hideously printed shirts?"

He orders two margaritas and a whiskey, then turns his attention back to me. "That's more my day attire."

"Good to know."

"He's really fucking cute," Billie whispers so only I can hear. "And the way he's looking at you..."

I nudge her, needing her to be quiet because that's the last thing I need him to hear.

He slides us each a margarita. "We have the best cocktails in the city, and these are supposed to be the highlight."

"A little biased," I reply, arching my brow. "But thank you."

Taking a sip, the salt hitting my tongue, I have to agree that it's a pretty great drink. "It's good."

"Good? These are amazing." Billie beams, stepping out from the side of me to see Crow better. "This is going to be my new place."

"Bronte!" Cam calls out, running up to me from the dance floor and giving me a big hug. "I didn't know you were coming out tonight. Do you know I haven't stopped raving about the cake you made me? I think it's the best chocolate cake I've ever eaten. I was pissed when Crow ate the hugest chunk out of it."

"I'm glad you liked it." I smile, then introduce Cam to Billie.

"Is everyone who works at Fast & Fury good looking or is it just me?" she asks Cam, after downing her margarita and placing it down on the bar. "Next round is on me. What do you all want?"

"I think I'm good for now, Billie." I still haven't even finished my cocktail. Cam, on the other hand, decides to be her drinking buddy, saving me from a hangover tomorrow.

Crow leans down to speak into my ear, sending shivers up my spine. "Want to dance?"

"Ummm." I don't know if this is a good idea, for many reasons. In fact, there's a whole list.

He's my boss.

I have to see him every day.

He's in a biker club. Let's not forget that little tidbit, shall we?

He takes my hand. "Come on, show me your moves."

"Okay, one dance."

The words somehow leave my lips. Maybe because it's what I really want. Maybe it's the seductive music.

Maybe because I need something for me.

Once dance won't hurt, right? There's nothing wrong with a little friendly dancing.

Crow leads me to the dance floor, smack bang in the middle, and pulls me toward his chest. Not too close, but just close enough that it feels intimate. That damn cologne of his teases me, all of my senses clouding my judgment. Losing myself in the beat, I gently move my hips, a slow tease, while he moves with me. He's a good dancer, surprisingly. I like it when a man lets you guide the pace and doesn't try to overdo it. Less is more, and he seems to know that, but he still moves in rhythm, sensually so.

"You look surprised," he says, eyes filled with amusement…and a dash of heat.

"I am," I confess, boldly wrapping my arms around his neck. "Not only at the fact that you asked me to dance, but the fact that you actually can dance."

"I shouldn't have asked you," he admits, hands finding their way to my hips and squeezing gently. "At work I've put you in a 'do not touch' box, but now you've stepped into my other world."

I'm unsure what to say to that, but I see what he means. At work we know what we're supposed to be doing, we know what the boundaries are, but now we've left the safety of those boundaries. I recognize there's a heat between us, one that seemed to be an annoyance to him and one I tried to avoid, not that I lasted very long. There's some chemistry there, but that doesn't mean we need to act on it.

"You don't have to say anything, it's just a dance," he whispers, as if reading my mind, spinning me around and pulling me back against his chest, this time my back pressed against him.

And he's right; it could be just a dance.

A dance that made time stand still.

I could walk away from here, from him, and pretend this never happened, and we could go back to work on Monday and act like we have been.

The song comes to an end, his fingers leaving my body, my arms lowering, but our gazes remain locked. I don't know what it is about him. It's much more than his looks—I know because I feel our connection in my chest, not just farther south.

I mean, I feel it there, too, but that's not all there is.

Flashing him a small smile, I take his hand and lead him back to the bar, where Cam and Billie are doing Patrón shots.

"I left you alone for five minutes," I say to them both, Billie sliding me a shot in response.

"We were feeling a little parched after watching that grinding on the dance floor," she says, wiggling her brows at me. "My, my, Bronte, I don't think I've seen those moves in a long time. Not since high school."

My best friend has no filter, and it's a fucking problem.

I turn to Crow. "Another dance?"

Apparently I don't even need to be drunk to make bad decisions.

Chapter Six

"I can't remember where I live," Billie murmurs, sticking her head out the window like a dog.

"Lucky for you, I know where you live," I assure her, glancing to the back seat at her and Cam, who is fast asleep. I turn back to Crow. "I'm assuming you know where Cam lives?"

He nods and rolls down his window, letting some fresh air in. "Yeah, we're almost there."

"Bet you didn't expect to turn into designated driver tonight," I say in a dry tone, closing my eyes as the breeze hits my face.

"Well, when I saw where the two of them were headed, I knew it was probably a good idea to stop after my one whiskey. We told Cam to come out tonight and check out the opening so we could buy her birthday drinks, so I was always going to make sure her ass got home safely," he explains as I study his profile. "At least she had a good night."

"Yeah, I don't know who was the bad influence out of the two of them."

"Definitely not me," Billie pipes up from behind,

sitting back in her seat. "I had such a good night tonight. I love all of you guys. Bronte, you getting fired was the best thing that ever happened to both of us."

Crow's lips kick up at the corners. "Never a dull moment."

"You have no idea." I laugh, looking out the window. "So now do you have to share your time between the garage and the bar?"

"Yeah, most probably," he replies, glancing over at me. "I'll go wherever Temper needs me. But the garage is my baby, always has been. Renny is the mastermind behind Kamikaze, so he's the one that's going to be in charge of it. They were all here tonight, but they were up in the VIP room."

"Watching everything?" I ask, eyes going wide. Great, I haven't even met his friends, besides Temper, and now they've seen me dirty dancing with Crow.

Crow chuckles, apparently not ashamed at all. "Yep."

"I guess they've probably seen much worse," I mutter under my breath.

Much, much worse.

"You're cute" is all he replies with, shaking his head, tone amused. He must think I'm so innocent, and I guess to their standards maybe I am. Still, the women I've so far met who are connected to the MC—Cam, Skylar and Abbie—are awesome chicks and I don't feel out of place.

That reminds me. "I'm seeing Abbie and the girls for lunch tomorrow."

"You coming to the clubhouse?" he asks, pulling into the driveway of a modern-looking block of units.

"No, we're meeting at a café. Why?"

"Just asking. Cam's is the one on the right," he says, parking the car and getting out to help her. He opens her door and lifts her in his arms like she weighs nothing, and closes the door behind him.

"I like him," Billie says as we watch him put Cam down in front of her door. She wakes up and starts digging in her bag for her keys.

"Do you now," I reply, turning back. "Is sober you going to share the same opinion?"

She nods. "I wasn't drunk when I first met him. Just tipsy. Anyway, I'm pretty sure drunk me makes better decisions than sober me."

"That's saying something," I laugh, reaching out and pushing her hair off her face. "You're going to have a hell of a hangover tomorrow."

"Worth it," she says, closing her eyes, lips tipping up at the corners. "It's been a long time since I had such a good night out. You know, I always have a good time with you, even though you never get smashed like the rest of us."

Crow gets back in the car. "One down."

"Is she going to be all right?" I ask him, staring at the front of her unit.

"Yeah, she just needs to sleep it off. I gave her some Tylenol and water," he explains as he gets back on the road. "Now where is Billie's place?"

"I might just take her back with me to mine," I say, and give him the directions to my apartment. There's a tension between us, and I know it's because the lines are getting blurred, and we have no idea what we're doing or where we stand. "Thank you for getting us all home, Crow."

"You're welcome," he replies, gaze caressing me.

"Why did you ask if I'm coming to the clubhouse? Are people who aren't members allowed in there?" I ask.

"If we trust you, you're allowed in there, yes," he says softly. "And I was just curious if I was going to be seeing you there tomorrow."

"Do you want to?" I ask boldly.

The car smells like him, and it must be addling my brain. Would I really walk into a biker clubhouse? I mean, I trust Abbie, at least my gut tells me I can trust her. I still don't know her very well, though, and neither do I know the man sitting next to me. I work for him and his club, and that relationship should be kept very professional.

Says me as I sit in his car after a night out.

It's clearly easier said than done, especially when they are all one big family and hang out all the time. Do I even want to keep myself separate from that?

Crow laughs under his breath, and reaches over and takes my hand. "That's a dangerous question, don't you think?"

I pointedly look down at our now intertwined fingers. "Says you as you hold my hand."

"Yeah, well," he grumbles, "apparently my life was much simpler before you walked through those doors."

"Is that why you acted like I was a pain in the ass from the get-go? I kept hearing and seeing how you were with everyone else yet with me your guard was right up. It was infuriating," I admit.

"I don't know," he replies, shrugging those broad shoulders of his. "You being there in my space just had me on edge and I couldn't figure out why. And I couldn't stop looking at you; it was damn distracting. And to be honest, I've watched the brothers fall one by one, and fuck if I don't want to be next."

"Fall?"

"In love."

"I see," I murmur, clearing my throat. Okay, so not ready to go there yet.

We keep chatting until we're stopped at the front of my place. Billie is fast asleep in the back, and before I shake her awake, I undo my belt and turn to Crow.

"I had fun tonight," I say, locking gazes. "It was unexpected, but fun."

"Me too," he murmurs, gently reaching out his finger and touching my cheek. "So beautiful you are, Bronte."

Smiling widely, I lean forward, hoping that he might do the same and kiss me. I've never wanted a kiss more in my life, and I hope he can't tell that by looking in my eyes. But at the same time I hope he gets the hint and gives me what I want.

He does, leaning forward. My eyes are about to shutter closed when his phone, which is sitting up in the drink holder between us, starts to ring, a name lighting up: HEIDI.

Who the hell is Heidi?

Either way the moment is ruined, especially at the thought of him having a girlfriend, or maybe just someone he's seeing or sleeping with at the moment. Maybe it's the reality check I need right now. Crow has heartbreaker written all over him, and I need to get my ass inside.

"Thanks for the ride," I say, get out the car, wake Billie up and drag her inside. I don't look back at the car, at him, and when I'm safely in the apartment I lean against the door and close my eyes, my head falling back on the hard wood.

Fuck.

The next day at lunch with Abbie, I want to ask about Crow and find out everything I can on him, but I don't. I'm here to spend time with Abbie and get to know her more, and I'm not going to waste that on a man who is potentially right now screaming someone called Heidi's name.

"I heard you were spotted at Kamikaze last night," she says before she takes a sip of warm coffee. "You should have told me, I would have met you out."

"I didn't know I was going to Kamikaze until I was there," I explain, telling her the story of how I accidentally ended up there.

She puts her mug down, eyes alight with humor. "That's hilarious. Temper said he saw you there, dancing with Crow. You going to tell me what's going on?"

Well, she brought him up, not me.

"Nothing," I say quickly, a little too quickly.

Abbie arches her brow, waiting for a further explanation, probably the truth this time.

"I mean, I have no idea. There's something there between us, but I think we both know it's going to be a bad idea to act on it. We've been circling each other at work, Crow has been an asshole at times, making me think he didn't even like me at times, if I'm being honest. Like he's fine with everyone else, but with me he goes from chill to broody instantly. Yet at the same time there's some weird connection, and this is the first time I'm admitting this out loud."

"Interesting. In the entire time I've known Crow, I've never seen him with a girlfriend," she says, tapping a black manicured fingernail against her chin.

"Okay, so he's not the commitment type," I mutter, pursing my lips.

Crow is a ladies' man. I knew that from the second I saw him, because he is so damn confident, calm and good looking, there is no way in hell he doesn't attract women.

Hell, it attracted me.

"Well," she replies, wrinkling her nose. "I mean, he's a Knight. It's never going to be a problem for them to get a woman, okay?"

"Great."

"But that doesn't mean they can't commit and be faithful. It just means they like to have fun when they are single, and there's nothing wrong with that. No slut shaming in 2020."

"You calling Crow a slut?" I tease, laughing back when she does the same.

"I never said that," she says, raising her hands in the air. "He's just a very…friendly guy."

I cover my face with my hands. "Exactly. Except with me he was standoffish at the start and it threw me off. But then last night we actually spoke and hung out—"

"And dirty danced."

"Yes, and danced." I sigh, staring down at the cake on my plate and wishing it would solve all my problems. "And I don't know where we stand, but work is probably going to be awkward tomorrow, so I'm looking forward to that."

"So, nothing, right?" she teases, using my original statement against me.

"Nothing." I nod.

"He's a really nice guy," Abbie says after a few moments. "He is used to taking care of everyone. He was a prospect when Skylar came into the Knights' world and was 'assigned'"—she uses air quotes—"to watch her and keep her safe when Saint wasn't around. That included Izzy and me as well, so us women are a bit protective of him. He's one of the good ones."

"Prospect?" I ask with a wrinkle in my brow.

Abbie looks at me in confusion for a second before understanding what I was asking. "Oh, that means he wasn't officially a member of the Knights. He was pledging, or whatever the boys call it. He was on probation."

"Got it. But he's now a member?"

"Yes. And honestly, Bronte, you have nothing to

worry about with him. He never has anything bad to say about anybody. He's just one of those easygoing, nothing-fazes-him types."

"Not around me. He was broody as shit."

"That's because you're different, and I don't think he knows how to handle it," she states, pushing her coffee away and bringing the lemon cake closer to her. "And I don't think you do either."

I've had a few boyfriends in my time. Nothing amazing and no one really worth mentioning, but I'm not completely inexperienced. But she's right.

I have no fucking idea how to handle this situation.

"He's my boss, and I actually really love this job and all the people I work with. I take it seriously, you know? Getting involved with a boss is never a good idea. I think we should all let it go, because these things usually don't end well."

"Technically Temper is your boss, not Crow," Abbie adds, lip twitching. "I mean, Temper is the actual owner of the garage. Crow just runs it."

Did she just find a loophole for me?

"We almost kissed last night," I confide to her, feeling the heat rush to my cheeks. "I wanted him to kiss me, and then he was leaning in…"

"And what happened?" she asks, sitting up straighter in excitement.

"His phone rang and a woman's name popped up, so I got the hell out of there, and that was how the night ended." I wince, puffing out a deep breath.

"What was her name?" she asks, bringing her face closer to mine.

"Heidi."

She blinks slowly a few times. "Heidi is Crow's sister."

Fuck.

Chapter Seven

After spending three hours with Abbie discussing everything from our childhoods to our friends to her dad, I decide to drive over to surprise my own dad. I haven't seen him since the barbecue, and although we spoke on the phone the other night, I know it's not the same. I'm his only child and I need to remember that he's not getting any younger. I should make sure I spend time with him.

I put the new Eminem album on for the drive, only turning the volume down when I pull up in his driveway. When I get to the front door, I knock a few times, but he doesn't open up. I know he's home, though, because his car is here.

"Dad?" I call out, knocking on his window this time, but nothing. Maybe he's in the shower.

"Let's see," I murmur, reaching up to one of the potted plants that hangs on his porch. "Bingo."

Some things never change.

Key in my hand, I unlock the door and step inside. "Dad!" I call. "Your favorite daughter is home!"

Nothing.

Thinking he must be in the bathroom, I open the fridge and scan its contents before settling on some green grapes straight out of the bag. I pop a few in my mouth and close the door with my hip before I call his name again.

Seeing his bedroom door slightly open, I push it the rest of the way and step inside, my eyes adjusting to the darkness.

"Dad?" I ask, turning the light on. My eyes go straight away to his bed.

When I see him there, unmoving, my heart stops.

He looks like he's sleeping, only...not. I've seen him asleep before, but this time he's so still. Unnaturally still.

I've never been more scared in my life, and I just hope and pray that he is okay.

Please let him be okay.

"Dad?" I say again, stepping toward him, moving the sheet from his neck and touching his shoulder, trying to gently shake him awake. "Dad?" My voice becomes more frantic as the reality of the situation hits me. Big, fat tears fall down my cheeks.

"No," I whisper, shaking my head. My trembling fingers reach for my phone in my jeans pocket and I call for an ambulance.

"Yes, I found my dad and he's unresponsive," I say quickly to the man on the line, my voice breaking, and tell him the address. "No, he's not breathing. Please, come soon."

I hang up and search for a pulse, but I find nothing. No.

He's going to be okay. He *will* be okay.

"Dad?" I whisper, wrapping my arm around him. What happened to him? I don't understand. He's a healthy man, and there are no signs of blood or a struggle, or any visible injuries. I check him over, looking for any clues, but there's nothing. It just looks like he's asleep. My head can't wrap around what my eyes are seeing.

"I can't lose you. You're all I've got. Please."

I rest my head on him, and cry, my heart breaking with every sob.

I don't know what else to do.

The rest of the day is a blur, and all I feel is numbness. I know it's a defense mechanism, because there's no other way I'm going to survive this loss.

My dad was the one who got me through my mom's death. He was there for me, sometimes just sitting with me in silence when I needed him, other times pushing me to express myself and talk to him. I don't know how, but he just knew what I needed, and with him gone…

So is my strength.

No child should live through losing not one but both of her parents so young. I'm only twenty-four. I consider myself a strong woman, but grief…grief is something that can destroy me.

Closing my eyes, I picture his face the last time I saw him, when he came into work with a smile on his face and food for me.

I hope he knew how much I loved him. He was the best dad in the world, and there was no love like his.

The ambulance arrives, and I know what they're going to say before they say it. The paramedics give me a look of pure sympathy, and they all tell me how sorry they are.

I know they are just being kind and doing their job, but I don't want their sorrys.

I want the one man who loved me more than life itself back.

I place the pillow over my head to try to block out the loud banging.

Go away, I mouth, wishing whoever's at the door would just leave me alone.

It's been a week since I lost my dad, and a few days since they told me he had overdosed on pain medication. My dad was someone who rarely even took ibuprofen, so I don't really know what to do with that information. I've been thinking about it nonstop since I lost him, and the story I've been told just doesn't sit well with me. There's something fishy about it; I'm not buying it. I don't know, in my gut I know that it's not something he would do. I know I've been overthinking it, but I just can't seem to let it go.

I haven't left my house once in all this time, and I keep ignoring anyone who tries to talk to me. I already saw everyone at the funeral, which was all a blur. My uncle planned the whole thing, asking for my input and making sure to include me, but I wasn't really present. The only thing I can remember is excruciating pain and different faces with sympathy in their eyes.

After the funeral, I locked myself in my apartment, and everyone else out. I'm just not ready to face people again, and I want to be left alone. I've probably lost my job, but right now I don't care.

Anything that mattered to me before means nothing to me right now.

My heart is broken, and with the way I'm feeling I don't think it's something I'm ever going to recover from. I always thought nothing could break me, but now I know that's not the truth.

I'm a different person from who I was a week ago, and nobody knows me anymore.

Sitting up when I hear the scrape of my window frame being forced open, I get out of bed in a rush. My eyes widen as I stare at Crow sliding into my now-open living room window.

Is he kidding me right now?

"Did you just break into my house?" I ask, frowning. "What the fuck is wrong with you?"

As I look at him, I suddenly remember him being at my side at the funeral, talking to me and holding my hand. I don't think I said much, but now that I see him in front of me, I knew he was there.

"No one has seen or heard from you, and we're all worried," he says, taking a step closer to me. He rakes his gaze over me, as if making sure I'm okay. "You can't just shut us all out, Bronte."

"I just want to be alone," I say, sighing, tears filling my eyes.

"When's the last time you ate? Or showered?" he asks gently. "I know you want to be alone, but maybe what you need is someone to take care of you right now."

He comes over and wraps his arms around me. Kissing me on the top of my head, he whispers, "You will get through this. I'm so sorry, Bronte, and I know nothing will take the pain away, but don't push the people who care about you away, okay?"

I melt into him, allowing myself to be weak, allowing the tears to drop and my body to tremble. He lifts me up and carries me to the bathroom, like a child, and fills up the bath. I hang on to him, like he can fix this, when I know he can't. No one can. But he's trying, and that's more than I can do for myself right now.

When the bath is warm, he helps me undress and places me in the water. He doesn't look at me in that way, and I appreciate that. He leaves me alone in the bath and heads out. I stay in until the water is about to turn cold, then get out, brush my teeth and my hair, and make myself feel human again. After putting on my silk robe and wrapping it around me, I step into the kitchen to find Crow making some coffee.

"I was going to cook you something, but you don't have much to work with, so I ordered some Chinese food in," he says, sliding me over the mug. "How are you feeling?"

"A little better," I say. Physically, at least. "What would you have done if my apartment wasn't on the ground floor?"

"I got lucky." He grins, flashing his teeth. "Come on, let's go sit down."

We cuddle up on the couch, and I drink the coffee in silence. Crow lets me, and just strokes my hair and my shoulders, sending goose bumps over my skin. "Abbie is worried sick about you, and so is her dad."

"I just can't deal with it right now," I admit, placing the mug down on the coffee table and burying my face in his neck and shoulder. "Why did this happen, Crow? I've lost both my parents now. And my dad... he was... God. He was my rock."

"I don't know why it happened," he whispers back. "There's no answer to that, Bronte. Life is unfair, and bad things happen to good people, and no one can control that."

I cry some more.

"I've got you," he says, and I don't know why, but I believe him.

The Chinese food arrives, and I eat a proper meal for the first time in days. Crow cleans up my apartment and even changes my sheets for me. Where did this man come from? I shouldn't have to have him doing these things for me, but it's almost like I've given up on life.

I need to fight. I know my dad wouldn't want to see me like this. He'd want me to be strong, and to push through.

I just don't know how to do it without him.

"Thank you, Crow," I say as he comes out of my bedroom. "Thank you for breaking in here and...for everything."

"You don't have to thank me," he replies, sitting back down with me. "I promised your dad that I'd look after you, and I meant it, Bronte. I'm here for you."

My tummy is full.

My house is clean.

My heart is…empty.

But still beating.

And that slow, soft strum is going to have to be enough to save me.

"Hey, Nadia, could you please call me back when you get this message? It's important, thanks," I say into her voice mail.

Placing my phone down on my side table, I look up at the ceiling and know I have to push myself to get out of bed, and out of this apartment. Crow has dropped by for the last four days, making sure I've eaten and that I'm okay, and I don't know how I'm ever going to thank him for being here in my darkest hours. He was my strength when I had none, but now I'm going to have to stand on my own two feet.

After thinking about Dad's death, and how something about it just isn't right, I know I have to do something. I need answers. I need to give him justice. I need the truth.

I have a shower, get dressed in jeans, a white T-shirt and my white Nikes, and open my front door.

I take a deep breath before stepping over the threshold. This is me facing the world, instead of hiding from it.

This is me facing life without my dad in it, and boy, is it hard.

Getting into my car, I have a reason for pushing through, a purpose.

I'm going to find out what really happened to my dad.

And I'm not going to stop until I know the truth.

Chapter Eight

My first stop is Uncle Neville's house. While I'm waiting on Nadia to call me back, I'm going to see what my uncle knows, and to see how he's handling the loss. It's not just me who will be grieving right now, and I know it was selfish of me to just shut everyone out, but I did what I had to for myself at that time.

When I knock on the door, he answers straight away. "Oh, Bronte," he whispers, pulling me into his arms for a bear hug. "I've called, I've come to your apartment... Where the hell have you been?"

"I'm sorry, I've just been trying to deal," I admit, clearing my throat. "How are you?"

He looks away. "Trying to deal, too. Freddy was the best younger brother in the world, you know that?"

"He used to say that you were the best bigger brother in the world," I admit.

"I don't know about that," he murmurs after a slight hesitation.

We step inside and I follow him to his spacious

kitchen. Sitting at the marble bench, I watch as he makes us some coffee.

"I'm glad you came by," he says after a few moments. "We need to stick together right now, and I want you to know I'm here for you. Whatever you need."

"I know," I say, smiling sadly. "I actually did want to talk to you about Dad. I know it sounds like the grief talking, but I don't think he overdosed on pain meds, and that's what they're telling me."

I look him in the eye. "I want to know what you think, and please be honest."

"Bronte..." he murmurs, exhaling deeply. Yeah, he's not going to enjoy this conversation any more than I'm going to.

"The time for keeping things from me has passed," I say, wrapping my arms around myself. "There was something going on between you and Dad. I'm aware you were doing business together. Do you know anything that could help me find out what happened? I need to hear the truth, and you're the only one that can help me."

He studies me closely. It's the hesitation there that has me intrigued. "Bronte—"

"Don't you 'Bronte' me. I want you to tell me what you're thinking. Tell me what you know. Because I'm not going to stop until I find out what happened, and we both know damn well Dad wasn't trying to overdose. He wasn't even taking any medication that I was aware of," I fire back, gritting my teeth. I don't care if they found pain meds next to his bed. Anyone could have put those there. I know my dad, and I know in my gut that he's not the type of person to do something like that.

He sits down next to me, coffee in front of us both. He pours some whiskey into his. "It's complicated."

"That's not an answer."

"Bronte—"

"Whatever it is, I can handle it," I assure him, but he still looks uncertain.

There's something he's not telling me, and I need to know what it is.

"Okay. You know that all my businesses haven't always been…legitimate," he starts, tiptoeing on the subject.

"I do know that. Dad told me that you deal with some unsavory characters with your business deals sometimes," I reply, shrugging. "What does that have to do with this? Do you think they targeted Dad instead of you? Mixed the two of you up or something?" I don't understand.

"Your dad worked with me as a partner."

"Okay," I say slowly, dragging the word out. I mean, my dad always had money, and I knew it had to come from somewhere. "The construction company, right?"

"You don't make that kind of money in construction," he mutters, clearing his throat.

My dad never acted like he was rich. I always knew my uncle had money, though. Not because he showed it off, but I could tell that money was never an issue for him. He may portray himself as a farmer, but he was a wealthy farmer.

"And what exactly did the two of you do that's making you look at me like that?" I ask him.

His Adam's apple bobs as he swallows. "We...we were trying to get out of some of the deals and become completely legitimate, but it was a harder process than we had anticipated."

I've never seen my uncle nervous in my entire life. He's full of confidence, and he can bluff with the best of them. He's never been one to give anything away, but right now he looks uncomfortable.

"What aren't you telling me?" I press, looking him dead in the eye. "Just say it, please."

He bites down on his lip before he replies. "You're going to look at me differently, and I don't want you to ever think badly of Freddy."

"There's nothing you can say that will make me think badly of my dad."

"Okay. One of our most profitable businesses ever has been dealing in...narcotics."

Wait, what?

My mouth drops open. "So you're telling me... Dad was a drug dealer? You're a drug dealer?"

What the actual fuck has been going on this entire time that I had no idea about? How could I have been so blind? I've been living in my happy little world while these two have been dealing drugs this whole time?

He winces. "A little more up the ladder than a drug dealer."

Blinking slowly a few times, processing this, I don't even know what to say right now. I can see why he didn't want me to hear this little bit of information. I'm shocked, but I also feel a little stupid that I didn't know this about two men who are close to me.

My head feels like it's going to explode. I feel like everything I knew about my father is a lie. I'm not a do-gooder. I'm not one to judge my uncle and father for what they did to earn a living. Am I shocked that it was related to drugs? Yes. Do I love them less? No. But he lied to me. That's what stings the most.

I rub my face with both of my hands. "So how did this happen? How'd you both get into this?"

He sighs. "When I was young, I wanted to find the quick and easy way on making money. Your father, he was the hard worker. He didn't mind putting in the time and work and paying his dues."

I smile because that *is* my father. He was never afraid of hard work.

"So I started getting involved with less-than-legal activities, and drugs were one of them. Because I didn't do them, I found that I was able to have a level head. I made a lot of money in a fast amount of time."

"So you were never a farmer."

"No, I was. I had the farm for fun."

I give him the side eye and he laughs. "Okay, okay. I had it to have a legitimate business. But I did genuinely enjoy having the farm. I still do."

"So how did my dad get involved in this?"

He looks at me with regret in his eyes. "When you started having your health issues"—he winces a little—"your father came to me for money for your medical bills."

That's a sucker punch to the gut. "Me? My bills?"

My father told me not to worry about it. That it was fine.

"I gave it to him, of course. No questions asked. But you know your father. He never wanted a handout. So he finally asked me the question he avoided all these years."

"He asked you how you made your money."

Neville nodded. "So I told him. And he wanted in."

My dad was the sweetest, kindest man you would ever meet, and he was out there supplying drugs and making our city a shittier place? I don't know what to think, or to say.

"Does Abbie know?" I ask through narrowed eyes. He nods.

"And she has accepted it?" I guess, adding some whiskey to my own coffee and taking a long sip. I can now see why he needed something stronger.

"Yes, she has, but it's different with her. We only just met and the circumstances around that required her knowing," he admits, ducking his head. "It's my fault—I brought him into this world. He needed money and saw how much I was making. He wanted the best for you, Bronte. All the money he made, he put into an account for you. The house he bought? For you. I know it doesn't make it any better, but he wanted to make sure you wouldn't have to worry about money."

"I'd rather have him here than have money," I murmur, voice breaking. "I just want my dad back."

Drug lord or not, I just want my dad back.

"And I'm going to have to live with that guilt forever," I hear him whisper to himself.

I'm smashed by the time Crow drops by that evening. I can tell he's surprised by the way he takes the bottle in his hand and lifts it in the air, looking between it and me, his brow furrowing. "You're drunk?"

"Something like that."

He sighs, and places the bottle back down. "At least you left the house then. Unless they do alcohol delivery drop-offs now?"

"They do. That's a thing," I say, nodding. "But yes, I did leave the house. And it was awful. I went to see my uncle Neville."

His eyes widen, and it's then that it hits me.

Crow would know.

This entire time, he would have known about Uncle Neville and my dad. He hired me knowing I was the daughter and the niece of a pair of fucking drug lords, and they still hired me.

"You hired me, knowing I was a drug lord's daughter," I say, shaking my head. "Even though *I* didn't even know I was a drug lord's daughter. Isn't that funny?"

I feel like an idiot. They all knew this, except me, and it's *my* life.

How can they all know more about my own life

than me? The whole thing makes me feel so out of control, so powerless.

"Bronte—"

"You knew. Abbie knew. Everyone knew. I'm guessing the whole fucking MC knew. But I didn't know." I pause. "And I kind of wish I didn't know. No wonder he didn't want to tell me. I wish I could go back in time and take it back."

Ignorance is bliss.

Crow sits down next to me on the floor. "It wasn't my thing to tell you. It wasn't my place."

His voice is calm, and soothing. Patient.

I know it's not his fault, but that still doesn't mean that I don't feel a little betrayed.

"Your place is next to me, on this carpet," I mumble, resting my head against his shoulder. "Do me a favor, and don't lie or omit information to me again, okay? I'm not going to take it well. No one really likes looking like a fool, do they?"

Everybody wants the truth, especially when it has to do with them. But I know that no one wanted to tell me because it's not something to randomly bring up in conversation. *Hey, Bronte, so what do you think that your father and uncle are serious players in the illegal drug industry?* I don't know I would've believed them even if someone did tell me that.

But I am still allowed to be upset by this.

"You don't look like a fool," he assures me, stroking my hair. "You look like a good, honest woman, and one who has never even used drugs, never mind knew her family was dealing them. They didn't want you a part of this, and I'm sure you can understand why. They didn't want to taint you, and bring you down with them. What they did was their decision. It has nothing to do with you as a person or how they feel about you."

There's merit to what he says, but it's kind of hard not to take this personally.

"Hey, I tried marijuana in high school," I whisper, laughing. "It was just once, when I was going through my rebellious stage."

He laughs at that. "Sounds like you were a real bad girl."

"You have no idea," I say, smiling sadly. "Dad never found out. He always trusted me and thought the best of me no matter what. I could do no wrong in his eyes. You know what?"

"What?"

"I probably won't be able to have kids, and I never told him that."

Crow looks at me, confused by my random fact.

"I have a history of abnormal cells on my cervix, and I had a few surgeries to remove them. However, if they're just going to continue to grow back, my doctor recommended that I get a hysterectomy, especially since there is cancer in my family history. My mother died of ovarian cancer."

I refuse to look Crow in the eye, recognizing it's the first time I'm really talking about this with someone without blowing it off as nothing serious. I realize I've been withholding telling people the full extent of what is going on with me because I didn't want to acknowledge the severity of it. But now, after Dad's death, I know I owe it to him to face it.

"My dad knew about the surgeries and the abnormal cells, but I never told him about the hysterectomy I may need. I never shared that with him, because I knew he would have been so upset, and now he's gone and it's too late." I turn to him. "You're the first person I've told this to. No one is going to want me after I have a hysterectomy."

He pulls me closer. "That's not true. And there are other ways to have children. You could adopt or foster. It doesn't mean you'll never be a mother, if that's what you want. It doesn't have to be the end of your dreams."

"I know. There are other options out there, you're right. But, since it was just me and my dad, I've always craved that familial connection. Before Abbie, I didn't really have anyone who was blood related to me other than my dad and uncle. So while I know there are many other ways to be a mother, having a child of my own was something I always wanted. And now that Dad is gone, it's something I wish I had more than ever," I admit. "Maybe it's best that Dad didn't know, because he always wanted to be a grandfather."

"He sounds like a great man," Crow says. "I'm so happy that I got to meet him that one time and I could tell that we'd have gotten along."

"He liked you," I say. "He told me that."

"That means a lot to me, to hear that. Most of the best men I know are in the MC. We get judged and looked down upon, so you can't always trust what other people think. He loved you. You knew him. Yes, there was a side he kept secret to protect you from the truth, but that doesn't change his love for you."

"I know," I agree. "I think it's just hard to think about him having another side to him. One I never saw. If it wasn't Uncle Neville and it was anyone else telling me this about him, I wouldn't have believed them. That's how out of character this seems."

"I know. People are intricate. I don't know if you can ever really, truly know someone," he says, kissing my hair. "But you know if people love you, and have your back, and are loyal to you, and those things all mean something. Friendship and love mean something. Family is everything, the type made from blood or forged in loyalty. I'm really close with my sister, even though she's a pain in my ass. I'd do anything for her."

"Heidi," I say, feeling a little sheepish. "I thought she was your girlfriend or booty call or something."

"I guessed as much, but no, she's just my little sister, who was drunk and asking if I could give her a ride home," he explains. "Our parents live overseas, and we rarely get to see them. So it's just us here, and we look out for each other."

"That sounds nice. I always wanted a sibling," I admit, closing my eyes, my head fuzzy, my body warm. "I lost my mom when I was a kid, and now my dad. Maybe if I had a sibling it wouldn't be so bad."

"You have us," is the last thing I hear before I fall asleep.

Chapter Nine

"Hey," I say as Abbie and Sky walk into the café. I messaged them both and asked if they would meet me here. I wanted to have a private chat with them about everything that has been going on.

"How are you doing?" Abbie asks, concern and worry in her eyes. "We've all been so worried about you."

"I'm okay," I reply, shrugging. I mean, I'm not, but what can I say? No one would want to hear the depressing truth.

"Crow has been keeping us all updated," Sky adds. Not too updated, because they obviously don't know that I know the truth about everything yet.

"I went and spoke to Uncle Neville," I say, and with those words, I think they both know why we are all here right now. It's not to discuss my father's death, or how I'm doing—it's to discuss why the hell no one thought it would have been a good idea to tell me the truth about my own family.

"He told me everything," I continue, swallowing hard. "And I guess I just wanted to tell you both how damn upsetting it is to find out that everyone you care about knew things about your life, yet they didn't bother to tell you. You all knew that I didn't know, right?"

"Yeah," Skylar admits, her green eyes filled with regret. "We did, and we're sorry, Bronte. I mean, we didn't know about your dad and his involvement. But we definitely knew about Neville."

"She's right," Abbie murmurs, reaching out and touching my hand. "I know exactly where you are right now because I felt the same. And you're right, we should have told you."

Sky nods. "I guess I personally felt like it wasn't my business, and that it was between you and your dad and uncle, but you're right. If I was in your situation right now, I would feel completely betrayed."

"We're sorry, Bronte," Abbie adds, frowning. "I've only just met you and have you in my life, and I don't want to lose you. In my defense, I don't know how I could have dropped that bomb on you after us only just connecting. But I know how I felt when I found out, so I recognize how confused, hurt and angry you are probably feeling right now."

I appreciate their apology. It doesn't change how this has all played out, but it's something.

"You can't choose your family, or what they've done or how they choose to live their life. I've learned that you can just go by how they treat you, though. And I know from what Dad said they were on their way out of the business," Abbie says.

"I know, which must have pissed some people off,

right?" I ask, biting the inside of my cheek. "I just have this feeling there's more to this, and I need to know. I need to know everything."

For the first time they don't look at me like I'm going to break.

"This whole thing is a really hard pill to swallow by itself, and then knowing everyone was aware except me also makes me feel so stupid," I admit.

They both hug me and assure me that isn't the case. Sky tells me a little about her mother, Georgia, who I personally never liked, and her involvement with Uncle Neville and the Knights of Fury. She also explains her own relationship with Uncle Neville. She had no idea who he really was either, so it's almost like all three of us have this in common.

At least it wasn't just me who was completely fooled.

And yet here we are, Uncle Neville's daughter, stepdaughter and niece, all together, and none of us hate him.

In fact, it's the opposite.

"Hey, I got your message about your dad," Nadia says as I step into her office. She gives me a warm hug, then her hands land on my shoulders as she looks over me. "I'm so sorry, Bronte. I know how close you were with him."

"It's been a rough two weeks," I admit, embracing her once more and then sitting down opposite her desk. "But I'm here because I need your help."

"What do you need?" she asks, sitting down and

going into professional mode. "Whatever you want, it's yours."

"I want to find out exactly what happened to my dad," I say. "And I want you to help me do that."

"Tell me," she says.

"I don't think what I've been told is what really happened. My dad didn't take any prescription pain meds, and the pills next to his bed didn't even have his name on them. They had no label. And after finding out potentially he could have had some enemies due to the nature of his…work, well, it seems like an obvious answer that someone could have done this to him. The police aren't looking into the blood work because they believe there's no foul play."

I tell her about his secret career I had no idea about and how that could be a reason that people might want him dead. The more she knows, the more she might be able to help me piece this whole thing together.

"Well, I didn't see any of that coming," she says, jaw dropping and brown eyes going wide. "Okay, let's start from the beginning, and I'm going to write this all down."

"Already done," I say, taking out a notebook from my handbag and handing it to her. She takes it from me and opens it, scanning what I've written.

"And you're sure?" she asks, studying me.

I nod. "I know it in my gut he did not overdose on pills."

"Okay," she replies.

And then we get to work.

We make a chart, listing everything we know, and a list of everything we need to find out. We start doing Google and social media searches, and we try to piece together this thing, one clue at a time. It's like old times, only now I'm the client.

Every new idea can lead us somewhere, and nothing is discounted. No lead is too small.

We are going to get to the bottom of this, and I'm not going to give up until we do.

"I went and saw Nadia, and the two of us are working on finding out the truth about what happened to Dad," I tell Crow and Abbie that evening. I invited Abbie and Crow over for dinner so we can chat and I can catch Abbie up on everything.

"You can't just throw yourself into this drug world. It's not safe, Bronte," Crow says, scowling. He rests his elbows on his knees, studying me.

"Clearly," I mutter. Or maybe my dad would still be here right now.

"It's a dangerous game," Crow says, sharing a glance with Abbie. We're all sitting on the couch, a cheese platter in front of us. "Especially since we don't know what we're dealing with."

"We?" I ask, brows lifting.

"You think I'm going to let you do this alone?" he replies, sitting up straight and running his hand through his blond hair. "I'll make a deal with you: I'll help you do whatever you need to do, but you need to promise not to go running into situations that you have no idea about or aren't equipped to deal with, all right? I know that you're a strong, independent, badass woman, blah blah, but there's only so much you can do if you're in a crowded room filled with men with guns."

Is he telling me that he will help me, but only if he gets to control everything?

"You're a control freak, aren't you?" I fire back at him.

Abbie laughs, but Crow shakes his head. "I'm not. I just don't want you killed. That's fair, don't you think? Fuck, now I know how Saint, Renny and Temper feel."

"What do you mean?" I ask, crossing my arms over my chest. "And I never asked for your help, so you can't act like I have."

He throws his hands up in the air.

"We've got your back, Bronte," Abbie murmurs, reaching over and taking my hand. "What he's saying is don't do anything alone, we'll be with you. There's a smart way to do things, and if you're emotional, sometimes you can be a little reckless."

"I'm not going to do anything stupid," I promise them both, knowing I cannot take on some drug dealers on my own. "I just need answers, okay? I don't want to start any drama, I just want to know the truth. I'm not going to be able to move forward until I do."

"I know," Crow admits, scrubbing his hand down his face. "Okay, so what's the plan? How are we going to do this?"

"I'm going to wait and see what Nadia can find first, and then I'm going to go back and speak with

Uncle Neville and find out a little more about the family business," I say, flashing my teeth. "I want to see if they had any competitors, I want to make a list of possible suspects, and I want motives."

The old private investigator in me is coming out in full force, and I'm so emotionally invested in this, it's not funny.

"Does this mean you're not coming back to work?" Crow asks in a dry tone.

If what Uncle Neville says is true, I have enough money to not need to run back to work, but that money is drug money, blood money. I've never not worked and supported myself, and that's not going to stop now. "No, I'll be back at work. I wasn't sure if I even had a job still."

"Lucky for you, the boss likes you," Abbie adds, smirking at us both. "Do you want to come back to the clubhouse, Bronte? I think it's time you met the squad."

I think she's right.

My first thought is that they must only let good-looking people join the MC. Everyone is friendly enough, some a little reserved, but I can understand why. I'm being brought into their clubhouse, their safe place, and they don't even know me.

"It's nice to finally meet you, Bronte," Izzy says to me, her partner, a man they call Renny, by her side. I meet Saint and see Skylar again, and the mysterious Chains, Dee and Temper once more.

"You too," I reply, smiling at her. "I must say this isn't what I pictured."

The clubhouse is…homey. It's clean and tidy, and it has personal touches—lots of black, leather and a hell of a lot of space for all of them.

"I said the same thing." She smirks, glancing up at Renny. "I actually own a house down the road, although I seem to be spending more and more time here these days."

"That's nice that you have your own space if you want alone time though," I reply, nodding in approval.

"We're sorry to hear about your dad," Temper says. "Crow says you're out for revenge."

I arch my brow at Crow. "I don't think I want revenge. I just want the truth, and I think someone killed him."

"Okay, I'll bite. Let's say there was someone who set him up, someone who wanted him gone. Let's say he was killed, and they made it look like an overdose. What are you going to do to that person?" Temper asks, watching me very closely.

I cross my arms over my chest. "I don't think I'll know the answer to that until that very moment."

"Which makes you unpredictable," Crow murmurs, wrapping his arm around me and leaning forward until I look at his face. "And I don't like that."

"You don't have to like it," I say, lifting my chin. "And you don't have to help me. I'm sure me and Nadia can do it ourselves. I don't need—"

He covers my mouth with his hand. "It's too late

for that, I'm in. Look around you, we're all in. So stop running your cute little mouth and accept your fate."

Fate could have done me worse.

He removes his hand, and my eyes narrow to slits. "I don't know whether to thank you or to punch you."

He simply grins, his hair falling over his forehead, his stupid blue shirt matching his eyes.

"You're lucky you're cute," I add, glancing around the room to see everyone watching us. "What?"

Abbie shakes her head, smiling. "You're both damn cute, that's what."

Izzy and Skylar bring out some cocktails and a cheese platter for us to munch on.

"The way Crow looks at you…" Skylar says, moving closer so no one else can hear. "Are you two officially together? What's going on? He wouldn't have brought you here if he didn't want you to be his woman."

"Abbie brought me here," I point out, watching Crow speak to Saint. "And no, I don't think we're together. I mean, we haven't even kissed yet. Why has he not kissed me yet?"

"Maybe because you're kind of going through a lot right now?" she guesses, looking to Abbie. "What do you think? Why hasn't Crow made a move on her?"

"He's been looking after you. Maybe he's waiting for the right time. You've only just left your house," she reminds me.

"Oh my God, maybe he sees me like someone he has to look after, and not a hot, sexy woman," I say, just as Izzy sits down with us, another platter in her hands. "Maybe he feels like I'm his responsibility. He did see me when I hadn't showered in days, so maybe he's not sexually attracted to me anymore."

I look down at my clothes. I could have put in more effort. I mean, I'm wearing the standard jeans and top. I cringe when I notice my feet. I'm wearing my Birkenstocks with socks. Why did I not change my shoes when I left the house? Or at least remove the socks?

"This is probably why he hasn't kissed me," I tell them, pointing at my feet. "We've solved the problem, guys."

Private investigator of the year.

I touch my lip. When's the last time I got waxed? Great, I've all but let myself go. To top it off, I put on granny panties this morning and they have holes in them.

The girls laugh, which gets Crow's attention, and he comes right over to me. Maybe he noticed the horrified expression on my face, which I wasn't able to mask in time.

"What's wrong?" he asks, sitting down opposite me. "And what's so funny?"

"Nothing," I state loudly, sending threatening looks to the ladies. "Absolutely nothing. Would you like a chip with some dip on it?" I ask, smothering a Dorito in jalapeno hummus and shoving it in his mouth.

The girls laugh harder, and I don't know where to look.

One thing I do know is, here, right now, I forget everything that has happened, and I feel almost back to my old self.

Almost.

Chapter Ten

Cam all but runs over when she sees me. "Oh my God, Bronte."

"Hey, I'm back," I say, hugging her and laughing as she picks me up in the air.

"I didn't know if you were going to come back or not. I can't believe what you've been through," she says, putting me down and cupping my face with her hands.

When I saw Billie last night, she told me that she and Cam have been hanging out together since the night we went to Kamikaze. I'm not surprised since the two of them seemed to hit it off so well.

"I didn't know either," I admit. "But I didn't get fired, so here I am. What have I missed? Who has been filling in for me?"

"Everyone has been pitching in. Abbie actually came in a few times, and whenever I haven't had any bikes to work on, I've been manning the front," she says, sitting down at the desk and showing me the schedule. "Luckily it hasn't been too busy for once, so we've made do. How are you? If there's anything I can do for you, please let me know."

"I'm…okay," I say, nodding. What else can I say? I'm never going to fully get over the loss of my father, and I know that. But I am going to have to learn to live with it, and hopefully over time the pain will lessen. Time heals everything, right? I might not fully believe that in this case, but it does give me a little hope.

Things won't always be this bad.

"When I was in prison I lost someone really close to me, and I know how hard it is. I'm here for you if you need me," she says, winking at me.

"I appreciate that, Cam. So, you never told me what you went to prison for."

"You never asked." She grins. "I was in there for stealing cars and motorcycles. Ironic, isn't it?"

She walks away, my mouth left open.

I spend the next hour catching up on the admin work for the business, organizing the receipts and folders, which have all gone to hell in my absence.

Crow appears around lunchtime with his hands full of food. "I brought you lunch."

"That's cute. What did you bring?" I ask, peeking into the bag.

"There's this nice Italian place close by, so I went in to get something for you but ended up ordering a shitload of food," he says as he sets it all out on my desk. "Take your pick."

"What a nice boss you are," I say, choosing the

carbonara. "Thank you. I'm actually starving. Seems my appetite has come back."

"Good," he murmurs, then calls Cam. We all sit around my desk, like it's the new hangout spot.

"Are you going to bring Bronte lunch every day now? Can we put orders in?" Cam jokes, opening her mouth and dropping a strand of spaghetti in.

"Maybe I'll start taking her out for lunch and leaving you to handle the workload," Crow teases her, throwing a plastic fork in her direction.

She ducks and laughs. "Can't be showing favorites now, boss."

Abbie drops in, sitting on my desk. "Looks like I arrived at just the right time."

"Do any of you work?" Temper asks as he follows behind her.

"I'm *at* work," I point out, twisting my fork into the pasta. "That's something, right?"

"More than we can say," Abbie says, grinning. She pats the spot next to her. "Come on, chill with us."

"If I sit there I'm going to break that desk," he murmurs, rubbing his hand over his head. "I actually came here to speak to you about something, Crow."

The two of them head out front to discuss whatever club matters, leaving the rest of us to finish our meal in peace.

"So has it happened yet?" Abbie asks me, wiggling her eyebrows. "Have you kissed?"

Cam's head snaps up. "You two haven't kissed yet? I'd have thought by how comfortable you both are with each other you'd already boned."

"Thanks for bringing this up at lunch, Abbie," I say in a dry tone, rolling my eyes. "Now everyone knows my business. Oh look, they're coming back, everyone shut up. Crow and his professional mouth will kiss me when they are ready."

Everyone starts losing it laughing, and then I have Crow asking what's so funny, to which I have no answer.

"I'm just really funny," Cam states with a straight face.

Crow looks at us all like we're crazy. "Okay then. I have to head off now, but I'll be back later this afternoon, all right?"

"Okay," I reply.

He flashes me a warm smile and then leaves with Temper.

"He didn't even give you a hug," Cam blurts out, wrinkling her nose. "Maybe he's broken."

"Bronte and her Birks and socks broke him," Abbie teases, laughing at her own joke.

I nudge her with my foot. "I'm going to kill you."

We all head back to work, and I'm left pondering everything they've said. I know Crow is interested in me, but he obviously feels like now is not the time for anything to progress. And you know what? He's right. I'm not in the best place right now, and maybe he's looking at this whole thing from a more mature angle. My goal right now is to find my father's killer, and that's what I need my attention on.

I don't need any distractions.

Still, I want him to want me, to be unable to stop himself from kissing me.

It should trump all of his common sense.

Maybe he's thinking the same about me, though, and waiting for me to make the first move. It's 2020 after all, and I'm the one who is all over the place right now. He's probably just being a gentleman, and I'm completely overreacting. I have been known to do that, and I'm sure most people can relate.

Crow and I will kiss when we're ready.

I'm on the phone when Crow and Temper return. It's almost closing time, and I'm heading straight over to see Nadia after this.

"Hey, babe," Crow says, squeezing my shoulders from behind as I sit at my desk, and kisses my cheek.

"Hey," I reply, spinning around to face him. "I had a call today from a man wanting a bike as soon as possible, but I told him there's a four-month wait. And he wasn't happy. I wrote down his name and number."

Crow looks at the name and shrugs. "Unless he's a Knight, he has to wait just like everyone else. Don't worry about it, I'll call him tomorrow. And if he or anyone else gives you a hard time again, tell me and I'll handle it, all right?"

"Okay. There's also a reporter that wants an interview and to do a feature on you guys for their motorcycle magazine. You have to call them back, too. And I did the new parts order and sent that off, and I finished sorting all the receipts for the accountant," I add.

"How did we run this place without you?" he asks.

"I have no idea," I admit, and then blurt out, "Why haven't you kissed me yet?"

So much for being patient and waiting until it just happened.

His eyes widen. "I was waiting for the right time."

"Oh."

"I had no idea you were waiting for it." Crow chuckles, moving closer to me. After looking up at him through my lashes, I drop my gaze to his soft, very kissable lips.

"I mean, I wouldn't say no" is my eloquent reply, before he lowers himself to his knees, cups my face with his hands and presses his lips against mine. Cam and Abbie walk in and start cheering and catcalling, but the sound of them is just background noise. All my senses are on Crow, his scent, the taste of his lips. The sensation of his thumb rubbing across my cheek.

When he pulls back, I feel dizzy, the butterflies in my stomach are out of this world, and I'm lost in those blue eyes.

"You have been through a lot, and I was just waiting until the timing was right," he says against my lips, kissing me again.

"Anytime is the right time," I say when I find my words.

It was the best kiss I've ever had in my life.

The kiss.

And boy, was it worth the wait.

I grab Crow's face and pull him back down to me. He's not getting away that easily.

Another long, deep kiss, our tongues working magic, my legs pressing together of their own accord, unable to contain the way he turns me on.

"Get a room!" I hear Cam call out, along with Abbie saying, "We're still here, guys."

I don't care who sees.

Crow ends the kiss once more, a wolfish grin on his handsome face. "Bronte, fuck. You were so worth the wait."

He took the words right out of my mouth.

Chapter Eleven

I can't stop smiling on the way to Nadia's, to the point where my cheeks actually start hurting, but I can't help it. My first kiss with Crow was more than I ever imagined.

Nadia is busy with work when I arrive, surrounded by paperwork. "Hey."

"Hey," she says, lifting her head up. "So, I've got some good news, and some bad news."

"Hit me with the good news first," I tell her, sitting down.

"Well, I've done some research and I've started a suspect list just going by other drug dealers in the city and those in nearby turfs who might have wanted your dad and uncle out of the picture."

"Okay, that does sound promising. What's the bad news?" I press.

"There's not much information I can find about them. None, even. And there's nothing on your dad or uncle either. On paper, neither man has ever done anything illegal—your dad worked a normal construction job and Neville has several legitimate businesses he hides behind, one being a farm. I guess this is good news, really, because their tracks are so well covered no one is ever going to find out what they've been up to," she continues, going through a notebook in front of her, her curly hair covering her face like a curtain. "But bad news for us because it gives us nothing to go on. I'm not sure how we are going to figure this out. I've tried your dad's finances, and I'm going through the phone records now. We need to speak to your uncle, though. He's the only one who can help, by giving us inside information."

"I think you might be right," I say, sighing.

I haven't spoken to him since the day I left his house, and I know he's not going to want to willingly give me any information. One, because it's likely going to get me into trouble, and two, because it means letting me into this double life they've both been living. I know he doesn't want me to have any kind of involvement with that. Without letting me see this other side of him, though, I'm not going to be able to find out who really killed my dad. And I know my uncle wants that, too. I need him to let me in, but that also means I need to let go of any judgment, because that's not fair otherwise.

And I know that's why he's not telling me, because he doesn't want my judgment, but the time for pretense is over. "I'll speak to him."

"I'm here with you all the way," she says, kind brown eyes sympathetic. She closes her notebook and stands up. "You want to go and get coffee or something? I'll tell you about each suspect and all the information I could get on them. I have a plan. I just hope people will talk."

She's right. I need my uncle, because he's the only insider who we have a shot at getting to speak to us.

"Sounds good," I say. "Thank you so much for helping me, Nadia. It feels just like the old days, except way more personal."

"I know exactly what you mean," she agrees. "And you're welcome. What are friends for, right?"

We head out to catch up. "These men are good at what they do. Fake names, fake addresses, the whole shebang. It's going to be hard but not impossible," she murmurs as we sit down at a café and order some coffee.

"I know, it's definitely not an easy one," I reply, sighing. "But it will all come together. It always does. What is your gut instinct telling you in regards to the suspects?"

She points to two names. "These two are the ones that keep sticking out to me. They both live in the area, and I know territory is a big thing with drug dealing. So I'm going to research them first. And if your uncle can confirm any of them, that would be a big help. We can work down the list and anyone he is familiar with we can make a priority."

"That sounds like a plan," I say.

We discuss our plan of action before we each head home. By the time I get there, Crow is just pulling up at the same time.

"Where did you go?" he asks, bag of groceries in

his arms. Is he going to cook for me? First the kiss, now dinner?

Today has been a pretty damn good day.

"I went to see Nadia, and we went out and had some coffee. And now apparently a sexy man is going to cook dinner for me," I reply, wiggling my brows at him. I unlock the door and he steps inside after me, putting the groceries on the kitchen counter.

"Prepare to be amazed," he says as he pulls out all the ingredients and sets them on the table.

"I was already amazed today," I say softly, but I know he hears me from the twitch of his lips.

"Me too," he fires back, lifting his hand and resting it on the side of my neck. "Do you know how badly I've wanted to kiss you? Ever since I first laid eyes on you. The timing was never right, and then you lost your dad and… I don't know. I was waiting for you to be ready."

"And I appreciate that," I reply, resting my head against his chest and wrapping my arms around myself. "I like how thoughtful you are. It's really different. And unexpected."

He laughs. "Didn't think a big, bad biker would be so emotionally adept?"

"Exactly," I admit, lifting my face up to him. "You're just…more than I'd ever imagined."

He kisses my forehead, my nose, and then my lips. "You came out of nowhere, Bronte, but I'm glad you're here. You're more than I ever expected," he replies, resting his forehead against mine. "Now let me feed you. And then you can tell me what you learned with Nadia, because hell if you aren't keeping me up to date with this whole thing."

I grin.

He makes me rib eye steak with creamy prawns on top, potato salad and garlic bread, and I tell him what I learned today, and what the new plan is. "So I'm going to speak with my uncle tomorrow after work."

"Do you want me to come?" he asks, but I shake my head.

"No, this is something I need to do by myself." For the sake of my relationship with my uncle.

Crow nods, and doesn't say anything else, which I also appreciate. I know he's the alpha male type, but he should let me sort through all of this myself.

When I need him, I'm going to ask, because at some point I know I'm going to be in way over my head. But for now, with my uncle, I'm going to do this how I need to.

Let's just hope he's willing to cooperate and give me the inside information I need.

"What are you guys doing?" I ask as I step into work. They're all sitting around my desk watching something on my computer. Skylar and Izzy are also here, which is weird because I've never even seen them at Fast & Fury before.

"Nothing," they all say, a little too quickly.

I step closer and peer behind the screen as they attempt to shut it down. "Oh my God, are you watching security footage of me and Crow kissing? You perverts!" I start laughing at the sheepish looks on their faces.

"Abbie said it was like a damn movie, and we were sad she was here but we missed it, so we wanted to watch a replay. Is that so bad?" Izzy says.

"You two are so cute," Skylar adds, placing her hands over her heart. "This is just a whole different side of Crow we are seeing. And I'm sorry, but I don't regret driving over here, making a complete detour from work just to watch this."

I shake my head at them. "You should all be ashamed."

Abbie glances between me and the screen. "Well, we might as well all watch it once before we have to go to work."

I throw my hands up in the air.

"Don't look at me," Cam adds, grinning. "I didn't even know we had cameras in here. That's how much I pay attention. But I am glad I got to see that again, not going to lie."

Crow steps in and I call him over. "You guys can tell him what you're all doing here, you creeps."

"What are they doing?" he asks, giving me a hug and kiss before addressing them. "What are you doing here, Sky and Izzy?"

"We came to watch some important security footage," Sky replies with a straight face.

Crow seems to understand straight away. "You've got to be kidding me. You all need hobbies."

They smile at him. "You're both cute, and now we're invested," Izzy says, standing up and wrapping an arm around me and Crow. "Keep it up, guys. We think you're both perfect for each other."

"Thanks," Crow replies in a dry tone. "It's like having three extra sisters, ones you didn't want or ask for."

"You love us," Sky calls out as she follows behind Izzy. "We'll see you all soon!"

We all say bye, and then I turn to Crow. "We *are* pretty cute, though."

He laughs, and kisses me, giving the rest of them a live show.

I'm sure the girls will be in at some point for the replay. I think it's sweet how close they all are, and how easily they've accepted me. They really are a great bunch of people to know, and I'm blessed to have them in my life.

Biker women or not.

Chapter Twelve

"I wasn't sure if you'd come back to see me or not," Uncle Neville admits, gesturing for me to have a seat on his expensive beige couch.

"Of course I was going to come back and see you. I was in shock, but that doesn't mean I was going to pretend you didn't exist. You're family. And you're all I have of my dad now," I say, sitting down and waiting as he joins me. "I'm not going to judge you for what you do."

I knew coming here tonight that the only way this is going to work is if I let go of all the judgment. I'm not here to question his life decisions, I'm here to find answers.

"You want to know who could've killed him?" Neville guesses, leaning back and staring straight ahead.

"You don't think he overdosed either," I say, glancing at his profile.

He shakes his head.

"I'm working with my old boss Nadia, to try to figure out what happened to him. I think between us we can get to the bottom of it. Does this mean your life is also in danger? I don't want anything to happen to you," I tell him, wringing my hands as the thought hits me. What if whoever did this is planning on taking out both brothers? I mean, my uncle seems to be the one more in the lifestyle; my dad was just following in his brother's footsteps to make sure he was financially secure.

That I was financially secure.

"I've upped my security," he admits, bringing his intense eyes to me, eyes just like Abbie's. "Don't worry about me, Bronte. I can look after myself. Especially now that I know I've got to watch my back. Your dad wouldn't have thought anything of it. He was unprepared. Not many people knew of his involvement. It was mainly me that people dealt with."

"Tell me, please. Anything that can help. I won't rest until I know the truth. And I have the Knights at my back, and Nadia—I'm not just going into this alone and without a plan," I explain, because I know what he's thinking right now. He's wondering if telling me anything is the best idea, because I could potentially end up in trouble, hurt, or even dead, like Dad. And I understand he doesn't want anything to happen to me. I feel the exact same way about him.

He takes a deep breath before answering me. "We were trying to get out of the business, and a war started over our turf. I...control a lot of the drugs that come in and out of the city, Bronte. So with me gone, it changes a lot for many people. There are some players who want to be where I am right now, standing on top of an empire with money, power and control. Certain people don't want to see others on top, and there are repercussions of whatever decision I make. Lives could be destroyed. People will become enemies. Everyone was waiting to see what would happen next, but before we even made the decision, we lost Freddy. And now I'm wishing I never even told him the truth about me, because he might still be alive then."

I put my hand on his shoulder. "Dad made his own choices. He didn't have to join you, but he did."

"He said I couldn't trust anyone else, so he wanted to be at my back. And he was right. He was the only person I could trust. This world is…brutal. It's so sobering to take a good look at yourself, and to realize that because of who you became, you lost the person you loved the most in this world."

I swallow hard, emotion hitting me. "There's no point blaming yourself."

"That's nice of you to say, but I don't think I will ever be able to forgive myself," he admits, ducking his head. "All we can do now is find out who did this and then try and survive the grief. There are three main players fighting for the top. I'll give you their names, but I need you to promise me not to do anything stupid. If you need people, I have people. Backup, numbers, guns, whatever you need. Call me, I'm here for you, all right? I want to see this asshole gone, too."

Guns?

I realize now what Crow has been trying to tell

me: I'm way out of my league. I've never used a gun in my life, and I don't know what the hell I'm doing.

"Thank you," I say.

I need to reassess this plan, and work smarter, not harder.

I leave his house with a list of names, and I know if this list got out, there would be a shit storm, so I'm not going to share it with anyone except Crow and Nadia. I get home and have a long shower, and by the time I'm dressed and ready for bed, Crow still hasn't shown up. I've gotten used to him being around here, even though we never formally discussed it, and now that he's not here I miss him.

Where are you? I ask via text.

He replies instantly. At the clubhouse. Is everything okay??

Yeah, it's fine.

I type out, I just miss you, then delete. Then type out, Are you coming here tonight? Then delete that too.

It's so hard when you're at that stage. You know the one. We're both into each other but we're not a couple, so I don't want to act needy when he's not even my boyfriend yet.

You miss me?

I smile down at my phone. Trust him to just put it out there and call it like it is. I reply to him with one word. Yes.

Be there in thirty.

I am falling hard for this man.

Shit.

I don't think I've really ever fallen in love before. I mean, I thought I did at the time, but looking back, my past relationships have been nothing but lust. I've never felt like this before, and it's a little overwhelming, yet at the same time I'd fight if someone tried to take it away from me.

I'm lying in bed reading a book when I hear the knock.

"Hey," I say, letting him in. "You smell good."

"So do you." He grins, pulling me against his hard chest. "How did it go with your uncle?"

"Good. I have some leads, and we're all going to work together to try to find out the truth," I explain, telling him everything in detail. I don't know what to do with them yet, but I guess that depends on what Nadia can dig up and on what Crow suggests that I do with the information.

"This is good," Crow replies, nodding. "Keep me in the loop, okay? I don't want you diving in without us at your back."

"I know."

As I lead him to my bedroom, I realize that tonight everything seems different. He's stayed here before, but that was when he was looking after me. Now I'm in a completely different headspace, and there's no way he doesn't feel the tension between us. It's like the kiss we had flicked on a switch, and now the heat has turned up between us.

I haven't had sex in over a year, and let's just say I'm all shaved, moisturized and ready to go.

"What are you reading?" he asks, picking up my historical romance novel, a shirtless highlander in a kilt on the front. He opens to my bookmark and reads a few lines. "This is steamy."

I remove my silk robe, letting it fall to the ground. I'm wearing a red lace bra and matching panties.

When I want something, I go after it.

Crow's blue eyes widen, and the novel drops out of his hand. The book lover in me wants to yell at him for that, but the woman in me wants something else more. I'm a little distracted right now.

"Are you ready for bed?" I ask him boldly.

He removes his shirt, giving me a closer look at male perfection. His skin is so smooth, his abs so defined, I can't help but go over to him and run my fingers down them. "I like these."

Crow laughs and lifts me up in the air, then throws me down on the bed. He comes over to me, and straddles me with his strong thighs.

"Do you know how beautiful you are?" he asks, stroking my hair back off my face. "I'm so lucky."

"You're about to be," I tease, as he lowers his lips to mine, kissing me deeply. The fresh stubble on his cheeks is rough on my skin. My fingers running down his back, I moan at the taste of him. His bare skin on mine feels so good, and I'm so damn excited for what's to come.

We kiss for a long time, just enjoying each other, and it's such an intimate moment. It also means I'm extremely turned on by the time his lips move to my neck, and then lower. He helps me remove my bra, and my eyes flutter shut as he kisses and sucks around my breasts, and then tastes my nipples.

I hold my breath as he goes farther down, past my navel, stopping where my lace panties start. Placing his lips on the material, he continues to kiss his way down, stopping over my pussy, where he kisses just over my clit. Thankfully my panties come off next, and his mouth is right where it should be.

"Fuck," I grit out, teeth clenched as he continues to torture me, the pleasure so immense I can't stay still. Crow pins me down to the bed and keeps eating me, sucking on my clit in between and having me on the verge of an orgasm.

When he slides a finger into me the same time he sucks on my clit, he pushes me over the edge and I come with his name on my lips.

His pants are removed next, and I'm still recovering from the amazing orgasm when he gently slides inside of me.

"I didn't even get to have a proper look," I say, grinning.

He flashes his teeth at me, and pulls out as I sit up, reaching my hands out for him. I stroke his big length a few times, my eyes widening. "Okay, that's big."

Leaning forward, I take him into my mouth, tasting myself and not caring, and take him in as deep as I can. His moans urge me on, and I keep going until he's about to come, and then I stop, pull away, and push him back on the bed.

Straddling him, I slide onto his cock, moaning loudly, and slowly ride him until he comes.

He's not done yet, though, because he gets hard again soon after, and makes me come twice more with his cock alone.

I'm left speechless, satisfied, and extremely fucking happy.

"We didn't use any protection," I point out to him. "I'm on the pill, though, and I'm all clear."

"I'm all clear too—I just got tested," he says, so the two of us look at each other and both shrug.

"So we're good then," I reply, reaching out for him once more.

He laughs, but doesn't say no. "Give me a few minutes."

I give him two, and then his mouth is back on me and I'm in my new happy place once more.

Chapter Thirteen

"So something happened between me and Cam," Billie says as we sit in our pajamas, feet up on the coffee table with popcorn in our hands. She has colored her hair back to its natural shade, a dark brown just like my own.

"What?" I ask, my head turning.

I haven't seen Billie much since I lost Dad, so I made an effort to invite her over. She knew my dad well, so it's harder seeing her than those who never even met him. She used to sleep at my house all the time, and Dad would make us bacon pancakes in the morning and then take us wherever we wanted to go. He always had so much time for me, and the memories with him will stay with me forever.

"We made out," she says, licking her fingers. "And did…some other stuff."

"I have to admit, I'm not that surprised. The two of you hit it off really well."

And I knew Cam was bisexual. Billie experimented in her younger days, although she's only dated men.

"That's all you're going to say?" she deadpans, looking a little confused.

I don't know what reaction she expected to get from me, but it's her life and I'm always going to support her no matter what.

"What do you want me to say?" I laugh, throwing a piece of popcorn at her. "Cam is stunning, so are you. Is it just hooking up? Like a distraction? Or is it something more?"

"I don't know yet, but I think it might be something more," she admits, picking up the popcorn I threw at her off the couch and eating it. "It's confusing. Women are confusing."

"Don't you start," I laugh. We share a grin.

"So tell me more about your hot sex with Crow."

"I told you it happened, and it was amazing, I don't know what details you're looking for, but—"

"Big penis?" she interrupts, getting straight to it.

I'm not one to talk about penis size and other things because I don't think it's really fair to that person. However, in this case I only have good things to say, so I just smile widely.

She gets the drift. "Damn, you hit the gold mine with that one."

"He's been my knight in shining armor through this whole thing." I pause. "Get it? Knight?"

She shakes her head at me, laughing. "Yes, I get it. Very nice, Bronte."

Moving closer to her, I rest my shoulder against hers. "Good things are coming for us, Billie."

"Or maybe they're already here."

Maybe they are.

"Cross this guy off," Nadia says to me, pointing to the first name on the list.

"Why?" I ask.

"Because he's dead," she explains, wincing. "I did a check on all the names, and number one was shot and killed in a drug deal gone wrong a week before your dad died."

"Shit," I whisper.

"Here's something else I found: there's a phone number your dad called a lot. I'm going to track the number, because it's not you or any other family member."

"Maybe it's one of their work colleagues?" I suggest.

"Maybe, but it's worth looking into. He spoke to this number for ten minutes on the day he died," she says, keeping her eyes on me. "I think it's the lead we need. We can't just walk up to all the men on the list and ask them, hey, did you kill Freddy? At least if we find out who he was speaking to so much, it might lead us in the right direction."

"You're right." I really did have no plan other than just to figure it out on the way, but this at least gives us something to go on.

When Crow gets home...I mean, to my house, I tell him about the phone number Nadia is tracking. We both agree that it could lead us somewhere, anywhere, and I'm now feeling a little hopeful.

"You know you can come to me if you need anything, right? We know how to track down numbers and people, too."

"I know," I reply, grinning. "But this is what Nadia does for a living, and the two of us work well together."

"I know that, but we're here if you need anything done…off the record."

"If I need something shady, you're the first person I'll come to, don't worry."

He simply grins, flashing his teeth. Sitting on his lap on the couch, I straddle him, my hand on the back of his nape. "So you're pretty *and* useful?"

Crow laughs, eyes gentle on mine. "Something like that. I even know how to cook and clean without supervision, can you imagine?"

"I thought men like you were extinct," I tease, kissing the tip of his nose.

"My mom made sure I was self-sufficient," he replies, then adds in a dryer tone, "Mostly by going traveling and leaving me home to look after Heidi."

In the midst of everything that has happened, I completely forgot about his sister. "When am I going to meet her?" I ask.

"She's gone on vacation with her friends this week. But when she gets back I'll introduce you to her," he says, kissing underneath my ear, slowly tracing lower to my neck.

"Hmmm." All thoughts of his sister and whether she is going to like me disappear right through the window.

"I missed you today," he murmurs, nibbling on my earlobe. He wasn't at the garage because he was helping do something at Kamikaze. Or at least that's where I think he was. When it comes to anything to do with the club and its business, the men are all very secretive. Crow doesn't tell me, and I don't ask. I think that's how it's probably always going to be.

"I missed you too," I admit, arching my neck for him, giving him more access.

He moans and stands, carrying me in his arms to my bedroom and laying me down. Lifting up my silk robe, he spreads my thighs and starts kissing the soft skin there. At the same time his fingers work the silk tie, opening the robe and baring me to him.

Raising his head, he watches me for a moment, flashing me a smile, before kissing my lips and working his way down. He pays attention to my breasts, sucking on my nipples, then goes lower, taking his own cool time. Always in control, my Crow.

By the time his tongue touches my pussy, I'm so turned on, my back arching, silently begging for more.

"Fuck," I whisper as his fingers dig into my thighs and his mouth works his magic.

My own fingers thread through his hair, pulling, pushing. I just need to come.

And he gives me that, his name on my lips as I orgasm, wave after wave of pleasure hitting me. He lies next to me, a smug expression on his face while I come back to myself.

And the second my mind is functioning again, I'm on my knees in front of him, repaying the favor.

"I just realized that I don't even know your real name," I say, both of us naked and sweaty, limbs tangled.

He makes a sound of amusement. "Xeno Crow."

"*Xeno*?" I repeat, eyes going wide. "Okay, I wasn't expecting that. So they just call you your last name. I thought there was going to be some epic story, like you once saved a crow, or you fought one or something, I don't know."

His laughter makes me jump. "You thought I fought a crow or something?" He pauses, and then says under his breath, "Maybe a raven."

"What?"

"Nothing. You're cute, you know that? There's no story behind it—Crow is easier to say than Xeno," he says simply, kissing my shoulder.

Bronte Crow.

Hmm.

"What were you just thinking? You have a weird look on your face."

"Nothing," I reply, leaning over to turn off the lamp on my side table, and cuddling into him. "You know, when I was drunk I remember telling you all that stuff about me, and how it's likely I'll never be able to have kids biologically. You never said anything about it."

"I didn't know if you remembered that or not," he admits. "But I meant what I said. There are other ways to have children. All that matters to me is that you are happy and healthy. We can worry about the rest later."

I'm silent for a few seconds. "I need to brace myself for the possibility of a hysterectomy."

"Then that's what you should do. We'll get through it together, all right?" he says, taking my hand into his, offering me his support. "I'll be here if you need me. Always."

Telling a man that I potentially can't give him children has been something that terrifies me, but Crow just makes it seem so easy, like it's just a hurdle, not a life-altering event. To some men, this would be a deal breaker, and a big one. I've never met anyone like him.

To him there aren't problems, just solutions.

He's incredible.

"That's a bold claim."

"I don't do things half assed, Bronte. I like you. I want to be with you. I'm fucking falling for you. I'm not here to play any games, all right?"

"I'm falling for you too," I admit, giving his hand a squeeze. "So I'm glad we're both on the same page."

We share a long, deep kiss, and it's meaningful. It's an acknowledgment that we're both in this, together. This isn't some relationship for convenience, or just for some sex. This isn't a situationship, because I've heard Billie tell me about those before: when you act like you're in a relationship but you're not.

We're both here because we wouldn't want to be anywhere else.

And there's peace in that.

"Goodnight."

"Goodnight, beautiful," he whispers into my ear.

Chapter Fourteen

Nadia calls me the next day with the name of the person my dad spoke to the day he died: Jean Turton.

I've never heard of this woman in my life, but a quick social media search lets me know she's in her forties and works as a dance teacher, salsa to be precise, along with various other side hustles like selling essential oils and massage.

Just how does she know my dad? I don't see any pictures of the two of them, but she could have them on a more private setting. Were they friends? Why did he never mention her? I know all of his friends, male and female, and he never once mentioned a dance teacher by the name of Jean. The whole thing leaves a bad feeling in my stomach. Maybe she was his masseuse, or he was secretly learning how to dance? I can't picture him having anything to do with essential oils.

I know exactly what to do next.

"I'll handle this," I tell Nadia. "I'll go to the studio and check her out."

"You sure?"

I nod, even though she can't see me. "I'm sure. I'll let you know how it goes."

"Crow?" I call out from my desk as I end the call.

He turns around from the motorcycle he is working on and stands, giving me his full attention. "Yeah, babe?"

"How do you feel about salsa dancing tomorrow night?" I ask. I already know he's a good dancer, so it's not like I'm dealing with someone with two left feet. I've never done salsa before, but this girl knows how to move her hips.

"Salsa dancing?" he asks, brow furrowing.

I explain what Nadia just told me, and he nods. "Salsa dancing it is. You ready to see these hips?" he jokes, doing a little dance move, just as Chains steps into the garage.

"What the fuck," I hear him mutter, shaking his head and walking into the back.

Out of all the men, Chains is the hardest to get to know, and he's barely said two words to me, which sucks because I know Crow is quite close to him. How, I don't know, but I guess Crow can get along with anyone, and that proves it.

Crow spins me around and dips me back, catching me off guard. "Is it bad I'm actually a little excited for tomorrow night?"

"No." I grin, wrapping my arms around his neck. "I am, too. Who knew being undercover and interrogating someone can be fun?"

"And what are you going to do if she recognizes you on sight? She'd have seen photos of you, surely."

He makes a good point. "Well, what is she going to do, run? Then we know she has something to hide."

Besides, it's her work—she can't just go missing. And frankly, I need the distraction right now, because this week I need to sort through Dad's house and decide what to do with it and all his belongings. I don't want to move in there—I think that would be too much—so I might rent it out. I want to keep all of his belongings, or at least most of them, for sentimental reasons, so I thought I'd rent a storage shed for them all.

"Maybe we should have someone in the parking lot waiting, and they can follow her after the class and see where she goes. We need more information on her."

"That sounds like a plan."

I'm going to meet this Jean, and I'm going to get some answers from her.

I'm also going to learn some new dance moves with the sexiest man I've ever laid eyes on.

After my shift comes to an end, Crow comes with me to Dad's house. My stomach is in knots as I step inside for the first time since I found his body in his bedroom. I don't think I can go back in there again. Crow has a look around, and stops to pick up a photo of me as a baby. I'm in my mom's arms, and she's laughing as she looks down at me.

"She's beautiful," he says, putting the frame back down. "And you are the cutest baby I've ever seen."

"Thank you," I say, a deep ache filling me as I

look at the photo. "She was amazing. And I think she would have loved you."

He doesn't look so sure. "I'm a biker, and you're a nice, well brought-up girl. You sure about that?"

"My dad was a drug kingpin. I doubt they could have used that against you," I joke, walking past him and picking up the next photo, one with all three of us in it. "And my mom never judged anyone. She wasn't like that. She was just a kind soul. It bit her in the ass a few times, but that was just who she was. There's not many people like that nowadays, those who like to give more than receive."

"That's true," he agrees, hugging me from behind. "It's nice to know that you think she would have liked me."

"She would have seen the stupid smile on my face and approved." I grin, turning around and looking up at him. "You've been nothing but amazing. I feel lucky to have walked through those doors at Fast & Fury, even if you were an asshole at first. Who knew getting fired would be the best thing to ever happen to me?"

"I'm fucking happy you got fired too," he admits, lifting my chin up and kissing me. "Now, where do you want me? Are we just going to box everything up? I know this isn't going to be easy for you."

"If you could do his bedroom?" I ask shyly, and swallow hard. "I don't think I can go back there."

All I can see is Dad lying here, not breathing, and me shaking him, trying to get him to wake up. It's like my mind wouldn't let me process it rationally, and I couldn't accept that he wasn't going to open his eyes and be okay.

"I'll do the bedroom," Crow says instantly, kissing my forehead. He puts some music on, which is a little distracting, and I appreciate that. While he heads into the bedroom, I start with the living room, packing up all of Dad's DVDs and entertainment items. He still has cassette tapes, all labeled in his handwriting. These are the things I want to keep forever.

My dad was quite the minimalist, so I go from room to room fairly quickly. Crow finishes up in the bedroom and then we both pack up the kitchen together. I try not to think about what I'm actually packing up—my old life here and my childhood. This is the end of an era for me, and a piece of me will always be here.

I find a pink scarf behind the TV, and it's not mine, so I have no idea whose it could be. Was it Mom's, which Dad pulled out from somewhere?

"We're almost done," Crow says as he sees me getting a little emotional. "You've been amazing, and so strong. But if you need to cry and let it out, that's okay too."

"How are you so wonderful?" I ask, resting my cheek against his chest. Lifting my head, I press my lips against his, and then get back to work.

Concentrate on the task at hand.

But it's hard to be productive when your heart is breaking.

"What did you want to be when you were a kid?" I

ask Crow when I find a piece of artwork I had made as a child of me dressed up as a doctor.

"It changed a lot," he admits, smirking at the memory. "But I wanted to join the military for a while there. I'm happy where I am now, though, so I wouldn't change anything for the world. How about you?"

"I also changed my mind a lot. It went from being a teacher to a doctor to a vet. The one thing I always wanted to be was a mother, though," I open up to him, smiling sadly.

"You still could be," he murmurs, kissing the side of my cheek.

I really hope so.

Once we've boxed up all of Dad's belongings, I leave them in the living room for them to be picked up and moved into storage. The stuff I want to get rid of I put in a separate pile to be donated. It's late when we get back to my apartment, and we take a long, hot shower together and then climb into bed naked.

"Thank you for all your help," I tell Crow, yawning and cuddling up against him.

"Anytime," he replies, kissing my temple this time.

I don't know how I would have done all of this without him.

It's like he was sent to me just when I needed someone.

And that is both scary and comforting.

The next day Crow hands me the pink-and-black helmet he bought just for me, to match the perfectly fitted leather jacket I'm currently wearing. When I told him I'd never been on the back of a motorcycle before, he got extremely excited, went out the back to search through all the merchandise they have to sell at the store, and picked these out for me.

"We are so going on a ride," he states, bouncing on his feet. "On your lunch break. I'll take you out for lunch."

Placing the helmet down on my desk, I shake my head at him. "You're crazy, you know that? And did you just take these?"

"Babe, I don't have to pay for shit here," he says, smirking. "We all just take what we want, it's just how it is. So those are yours, and I can't wait to have your arms wrapped around me and your breasts pressed against my back."

My eyes widen as I glance around making sure no one else heard that. "Can you not?" I whisper-yell. "People are going to quit because you're inappropriate."

"People, or you?" he teases.

"All of us," I say in a dry tone, but can't keep the smile off my face.

"They all saw the kiss, I don't think anything we do will surprise them."

"I need to get back to work." The phone rings, to make my point. "Fast & Fury, Bronte speaking," I say while looking him in the eye. He takes the hint, eyes dancing with amusement, and gets back to it.

When twelve o'clock hits, Cam takes over so I can have my break, and Crow leads me over to his bike.

"Meet my other girlfriend," he says, and I'm pretty sure he's talking to his bike, not me.

"Men and their toys," I mutter to myself as I put on the heavy jacket. "Now tell me what I need to know."

"Keep your feet on the footrests," he says, pointing to them. "Lean when I lean. Just follow my body and my lead. I know you're good at that."

I can feel my cheeks heat. "That's it?"

He nods. "You'll love it. Just enjoy the ride. You don't need to worry about anything else."

"Okay." I climb on after him, wrap my arms around him and hold on for dear life. The loud engine has me on edge a little, but once he starts riding, I kind of understand what all the hype is about.

There's a sense of freedom, of wildness, and pure satisfaction.

I like being pressed up against him, and I like watching the view pass us. This beats going in a car any day. Crow rests one of his hands on my leg, giving it a little squeeze, and I think it's cute. Even if he only has one hand on the handlebars right now, he knows what he's doing.

I like that, too.

We stop at a Sri Lankan restaurant for lunch, and when I climb off the bike, I take my helmet off and smile. "That was awesome."

He looks happy at my comment. "Thank fuck. I didn't know what I was going to do if you hated it. I love going for rides, long ones, short ones, I don't care—being on my bike is my happy place."

Stepping forward, I give him a quick kiss. "I can see why. Now feed me, I'm hungry."

He grins and leads me inside.

After lunch, we ride back to work, and I feel so relaxed and excited. It gives me time to think, to be in my own head with no interruptions.

Ten out of ten, would recommend.

Chapter Fifteen

When my shift is over, I get changed for the salsa class. I found a red dress in the back of my closet. Pairing it with some gold heels, with my hair down and some red lipstick on, I'm ready to play the part. Crow surprises me by stepping out from the staff room in a white shirt, black slacks and dress shoes.

"Damn, you look good," I announce, doing a circle around him. "A little too good. I almost don't want to take you out in public like that."

"That's my line," he murmurs, grabbing me by the waist and stopping me with my body against his. "You look smoking hot, Bronte. Red looks good on you."

"Thank you," I reply, batting my lashes a little. "We clean up pretty well, don't we?"

He twirls me and dips me back, kissing my neck. "Mmmhmm. I think we're going to be naturals at the whole salsa thing."

"We better go and find out."

Jean's dance studio is small and hard to find, located behind a factory. We hear the music as soon as

we get out of the car, and excitement fills me. I probably shouldn't allow myself to be so distracted, because we are here for research and nothing else, but
I can't help it. This is going to be fun.

Dee and Nadia are going to follow to our location
and park on the next street over. When the class is
finished, they are going to tail Jean and see where she
goes. It's a simple plan, but it should lead us somewhere and give us something to work with.

As we enter through the open glass doors, everyone stops to look at us. The class consists of mostly
older ladies and gentleman and they are all dolled up
for the occasion.

"Hello," I say as I scan the crowd. I recognize Jean
instantly, and from the surprised look on her face, I
know she recognizes me too. "We're here to join the
class. The ad said we could just drop in for a trial." I
try to keep it light and friendly.

She's quiet for a few seconds, but then catches herself. "Of course, yes, come on in. I'm Jean, and this is
our salsa class for all levels. Welcome to the group."

"I'm Bronte and this is Crow," I introduce, offering her my hand. She takes it, with a very gentle hold.
"We haven't done any dancing before, but we like to
think we have some rhythm."

"I'm sure you'll be fine," she replies, forcing a
smile and nodding toward the group. "Come and join
us."

She's an attractive woman for her age, that's for
sure. All of us could only hope we look that good at
her age. With her wavy brown hair, curvy yet slim

build and big, bright eyes, she looks like she could belong in Hollywood.

There's so many things I want to ask her, the first one being how did you know my dad, and the second being why haven't I heard of you? Dad never dated after Mom—he said there was no one else for him—but this woman has me feeling a little unsettled. Was it her pink scarf I found at his house?

We join the group, heading for the back, and follow the instructions she gives us. We start in a neutral position and then learn the steps, the loud music setting the mood. We get the step forward and the backwards hip and foot movements instantly, and she explains the timing to us. We practice for the next ten minutes alone before we join with our partner and try out the steps together.

As soon as I face Crow and he looks me in the eye, I start feeling a little flustered, and miss the first step. We start over, and this time we both nail it, moving in sync. It's just the basic movements, but it feels good to be able to do them.

"Told you we'd be good," he says, grinning. "We're naturals."

He swirls me around the way she shows us, then pulls me back against him. It's so easy to forget why we actually came here, especially with the sensual music and dance moves. I wish we were just here for the dance class.

When it comes to an end, I approach Jean alone and thank her for a wonderful class.

"You're welcome. You and your partner are great

dancers," she commends, but I notice that she avoids my gaze.

"Thank you. I think you knew my dad, Freddy," I blurt out, watching her reaction closely. It's a bold move, but I want to see what she has to say.

She goes blank. "I'm sorry, I have no idea who that is. You must have me mistaken."

My eyes widen as I realize she's going to play that card. "Yes, I must. I'm sorry. Thanks again for the class. I'm sure we will be back."

Lying can only mean one thing: she has something to hide.

And I'm going to find out what it is.

"I can't believe the hag just lied straight to my face!" I tell Crow, pacing up and down. We came back to the clubhouse to wait for Nadia and Dee, and I've been fuming ever since we left the dance studio.

"What if she spoke to him on the phone but never met him? Or maybe he gave a fake name to her?" Crow suggests, trying to be the voice of reason.

"Okay, so there may be an explanation," I admit, thinking those two ideas over. "But the way she looked at me and avoided any eye contact, come on! That's the look of someone who knew damn well who I was, and felt guilty about something."

I'm sure of it. My gut tells me this woman knows something, and I'm not going to let this go until I know for sure.

"Okay, babe," Crow says, taking my hand and pulling me to sit on his lap. "Whatever it is, we'll find out, okay?"

Nodding, I rest my head against his shoulder. "It's just frustrating."

"I know," he says as he rubs my back. "And I understand how much this means to you, okay? We will get to the bottom of it, no matter how many random classes we have to go to. Belly dancing? Cooking? Whatever, we will do it."

Laughing, I lift my head. "I love you, you know that?"

Yeah, I said it first.

I hadn't planned on it, but it kind of just came out, and I don't regret it, because I truly do mean it.

I'm in love with Crow.

How couldn't I be?

His smile couldn't be any wider. "I love you too, Bronte. You have no idea."

He kisses me, cupping my cheeks with his big hands, bringing me as close to him as I could physically be.

With my clothes on, anyway.

"Let's go to your room," I say into his ear just as Nadia and Dee walk in, seeing us all over each other and chuckling.

"So while we've been doing all the work, this is what you two love birds have been doing?" Dee asks, clucking his tongue in disapproval. "You both owe me."

"We do," I admit, climbing off Crow's lap and letting him hide his erection. Pretending I don't see it standing to attention, all thick, big and hard. "What happened?"

"We followed her back to her house," Nadia explains, sitting down on the chair next to Crow. "She didn't go anywhere else, so there's nothing fun to report there, but I put a bug in her car. So we're going to be able to track her movements and listen to any conversations that take place. I'm going to go back to her house tomorrow when she's teaching her dance class and put a bug in her house, too. I think that's where we'll be able to hear all the juicy shit."

I clap my hands in excitement. "Holy shit, I didn't even think of that."

Dee turns to Crow. "She has no idea who we are, does she?"

Crow simply smirks, which means he's probably thinking that I underestimate them, too. "Thank you, the both of you."

"You're welcome," Nadia replies, grinning. "This is only the beginning."

"Anytime," Dee says, fist bumping Crow. "Been quiet around here for a bit. I'm actually happy for the action. Anything else you need, give me a buzz."

"Thanks again," I say to both of them.

Dee winks at me and heads back inside, while Nadia waves and says she will speak to me tomorrow.

"We're so lucky to have all of them," I say, sitting back down on his lap. "And the MC, you really are like a huge, loyal family. I've never seen anything like it, especially with people that aren't related by blood. It's beautiful. Ride or die."

"You're a part of it now," Crow replies, placing his palm over my heart. "You have me, which means you have my boys. Whatever you give us, we give back to you tenfold."

"Except my body, hopefully," I tease, arching my brow at him.

Crow laughs. "Anyone touches you, I will kill them. You are mine. You were made for me, and as long as you want to be here, this is where you'll be. Right by my side."

His words excite me...and turn me on.

"Okay, *now* let's go to bed," I say, and bite my lip.

He takes the hint and stands with me in his arms, carrying me to his bedroom, closing the door and then pushing me back against it.

I never know what he's going to do, and it's such a turn-on. There's no predictability with him. I just know one thing for sure: he's going to make certain I'm satisfied.

And as far as I'm concerned, that's all I need to know.

Chapter Sixteen

"You look familiar," one of the customers says to Cam, who is having none of it.

"I used to do porn, so maybe that's why," she replies, flashing him a sarcastic smile and walking away.

I try to stop myself from laughing, but I can't. Still, I pull myself together as the man approaches me with some merchandise in his hands. "I'm guessing that's a no, she doesn't want to give me her number," he grumbles, placing the helmet and jacket down on the desk.

"You should try some new lines," I suggest, smiling. "But she *is* seeing someone, so they probably wouldn't have worked anyway."

"Noted," he replies, nodding. "How about you? Are you single?"

I blink slowly at the man, any sympathy I have for him being rejected by Cam disappearing. Do men really think women would take them up on an offer of being second place? Surely not.

"No, I'm not," I reply, placing his items in a bag. "That will be three hundred and seventy dollars."

He pays in cash and leaves without saying anything further, which I appreciate. Cam comes back out, laughing when I tell her what happened.

"Men are something else." She smirks, shaking her head. "Lucky Crow isn't here or he'd be leaving without a limb."

"And if Billie was here?" I tease.

"Probably without one of his nuts."

"So you two are all good then?" I pry, sitting back in my seat and wiggling my brows. "Exclusive, even?"

"Well, we haven't put a label on it," she admits, not seeming bothered by that fact. "I don't know. We're just having some fun. I'm just going to take it as it comes. Ha, as it comes."

"You're the worst," I deadpan, just as Nadia steps into the warehouse and beelines for me.

"Hey, Bronte."

"Nadia. What's up? Is everything okay?" I ask, standing.

"Everything is fine, I just have some information for you," she states, handing me a folder. "I typed out some of the conversations I overhead from Jean for you. I think you might find them interesting."

Eyes widening, I pull out the first piece of paper, and read.

"It's Freddy's daughter, Jasper, she knows something. I don't know what to do, I think I should leave town. Why else would she come to my studio? She knows."

"That snake," I murmur to myself. "Jasper. Where have I heard that name before?"

"He was on the list," Nadia says, crossing her arms over her chest. "He's one of the men trying to take over Grayson's territory."

"Who the hell is Grayson?"

"Your uncle Neville," she explains, telling me how apparently he goes by different names. Nothing my uncle does at this point is going to surprise me.

"So Jean has ties to Dad and to one of the men on the suspect list. What do you do now?" I ask, frowning. "Tell me what *I* need to do."

"I think we should wait and see what else she says," she says, looking down at the folder. "We need more proof and we need to know what their plan is before we go in guns blazing."

But it's not looking good for her. Did she kill my dad, or was it Jasper? Or both of them?

I read the rest of the conversations, but they don't give anything else away. I still don't know how she is connected to Dad exactly, and I still don't know what she wants.

But I will.

When Crow comes over that night, he lets me listen to the new recording. It's so much better actually listening to her voice instead of reading it.

"They are onto us, I know it," Jean says. *"I want*

to close the studio and just leave town. It's not safe for me anymore."

"Don't be ridiculous," Jasper replies. "You will do what I tell you to do."

"So Jean and Jasper are working together," I say when it comes to an end. "Maybe she's hiding something for him? Maybe it was him calling Dad from her phone."

"Maybe." Crow nods slowly. I know he wants to say something, but he's hesitating.

"What?" I ask.

He touches the stubble on his jawline. "I'm surprised you haven't come up with the most obvious conclusion, which is that your dad and Jean had something to do with each other."

My mouth opens and closes again. "My dad never dated anyone after my mom. He said he never would, because there was no one else for him except her."

I realize how ridiculous it sounds when I say it now, but I grew up hearing this, and believing it.

But then I think of that scarf. Maybe what Crow is saying is true. It's still a hard pill for me to swallow. I always told my dad I'd be happy for him if he moved on, but he assured me he was fine as he was. I even asked him if he was dating and he said no.

"At the end of the day, he was still a man," he says gently, stroking my knuckles with his fingers. "And everyone gets lonely, babe. Imagine being alone all of those years. All I'm saying is, you never know. With the amount of times they spoke on the phone, and for